MAGIC BLAZE

SEDONA VENEZ

WANT FREE SEDONA VENEZ BOOKS?

Sign up for Sedona Venez's Newsletter and receive FREE BOOKS. In addition to the free stories, you will also get special pricing, exclusive previews and news of new releases.

GET A FREE SEDONA VENEZ BOOK!

Join Sedona's mailing list to be the first to know of new releases, free books, special prices and other author giveaways.

https://sedonavenez.com/free-book

FROM THE HELM of my dragon's back, I truly felt like I could conquer the world. With the wind whipping through my hair, cool and crisp, filling my lungs with every breath, I was invincible. High above the rest of the world, I was untouchable, nestled between his dangerous spine spikes, holding tightly to him as his magnificent sunset scales caught the late afternoon light. Had we been returning to the Sanctius village for a happier reason, I might have really let myself go. Thrown my arms back. Screamed. Did a full Jack-on-the-bow-of-the-Titanic kind of thing.

But given that we were traveling back to Darius's childhood village because his father, Khalon Thomas, alpha of the Sanctius dragon shifter clan, had died yesterday, I didn't feel much like cheering and whooping. While he had kept his features cool and his posture sharply erect, my dragon's heart *hurt*. I could feel the sorrow dripping from it with each passing minute. But there would be no huge emotional outbursts—not after the one he had succumbed to just below the mountain peak, as my new family flew overhead with his younger brother, Quinn. While a chorus of dragon cries, cheerful and exhilarating, filled the skies, we had sat together while he cried, while he poured his grief, his devastation, into me, and I took every drop until the numbness hit. From there, Darius had resumed his responsibilities as big brother and next-in-line for the alpha throne, his storm-gray gaze steely and his mouth set in a hard, determined-not-to-quiver line.

While he would have preferred that I stay back to continue exploring the beginnings of new relationships with my family, we agreed to travel back to the Sanctius clan together.

Together, or not at all.

My father, Brisbane clan alpha, James Holloway, understood. My new siblings, Leda and Hudson, had appeared stricken at the passing of another alpha, instantly offering their sympathies and insisting I stay with Darius during this time. The gesture had surprised me; Leda had been so desperately keen to speed our friendship from zero to one hundred from the moment she met me. Yet she understood, without me having to say more than a few words, that Darius needed me.

Just as Quinn seemed to need Catriona. The news of his father's death had hit the middle Thomas son particularly hard. As the rest of us had returned to the Brisbane castle to make travel preparations, Quinn and my best friend lingered at the mountain's peak. I'd cast a look over my shoulder before leaving, finding Quinn with his head in Catriona's lap, sobbing. The sight had made my heart heavy, and I'd found myself fighting the desire to comfort him too. After all, he was my dragon's brother —blood, kin, friend. I just wanted to make the pain disappear, for all of them.

I had the training to do it, after all, despite not having seen any of my therapy clients in months. I'd known, however, that Quinn needed Catriona more than he needed my university degrees and background in grief counseling. Just as I'd known that Darius needed my unwavering, constant support during this transition period. Whether we spoke or not, I knew what he needed most of all was simple: he needed his hand in mine, knowing that I wouldn't let go.

So, even though there was no greater high than flying over the world straddling a dragon, I kept my shit together for everyone's sake. By no means was I an insensitive ass, but I'd dare anyone to switch places with me and *not* scream at the top of their lungs like they were on the most exhilarating, emotional, heart-pounding rollercoaster ride of their lives.

I glanced back and spied Quinn in dragon form nearby. Catriona had been too frightened to even consider clambering onto Quinn's back, despite the temporary saddle the Brisbane clan offered to make. Apparently, her brief scalding from touching Darius's scales had left a lasting impact, so my bestie opted to take the portals back to the Sanctius village. While Quinn had wanted to go with her, to traverse the magical portals together, she had convinced him to fly ahead and see to his family. In that moment, if for some ridiculous reason she hadn't had Darius's respect before, she had certainly earned it there.

Still, the odd mournful cry that Quinn released here and there on our journey out of Brisbane dragon territory was heart wrenching, and a part of me wondered if Catriona felt it too. Biting the insides of my cheeks, I faced forward and trailed my hand along Darius's thick neck; if we were separated, his heartache would weigh on me, just as I was sure Quinn's weighed on Catriona. With her fae speed and the effectiveness of the magical portals taking her across state lines, we all suspected she would arrive shortly after we did.

With no warning, Darius shot up into the cloud cover. I braced myself for impact, little bumps erupting across my skin as cold droplets washed over me. Before we left, I had finally mastered a sort of bubble spell that kept the flies and wind out of my eyes this time around, but I hadn't extended it to cover the rest of my body. I hugged him tightly, leeching the warmth out of his scales as we flew through endless gray, light above and darkness below.

We broke free from the cold about five minutes later, and I gasped, drawing in the refreshing air as the wind dried me.

Whatever it missed, my quick cast of a water wicking charm got rid of the rest. The Sanctius clan's mountain range loomed ahead, growing larger with each tremendous flap of Darius's wings. The village seemed to come to life as we approached, despite the fact it was shrouded in cloud cover and grief alike. Light poured out of the windows of the various halls scattered along the path up the mountains, and with my enhanced sight, I spied Cynthia and Hayden waiting for us outside the alpha's hall at the very top. Alone. They must have requested it to be that way; the last time we were there, people were falling all over themselves to be near Darius. It was *very* apparent that the clan adored their ruling family. The pain of losing Khalon... It would resonate through every home, down to the youngest child.

Darius slowed his approach, wings out taut and dragging in the wind—like any modern aircraft braking system. I admired it for a moment, then winced at his earthshattering bellow. It all but shook the village, the vibrations unseen in the solid mountain foundations, yet felt in the soul of every shifter present.

I tightened my thighs and braced for landing as Darius circled what was once his father's hall twice before touching down. While the Brisbane clan had used magic to enhance the natural beauty of their mountain summer home, courtesy, in large part I had learned, of my fae mother, the Sanctius village was mountain-born in every sense of the word. More than I remembered, at that. All the gray. The scraggly foliage. Harsh. Unforgiving. Yet as soon as I set foot on the slate rock, it was like coming home after a too long absence. I couldn't describe it. Even with the somber atmosphere, I knew in that moment that *this* was where I needed to be. Where I was destined to be. Not New York City. Not Alfheim. Here—with my dragon in his hour of need.

"Darius!" His mother's cry echoed across the mountain peak, a sob catching in her throat as she rushed forward. A soft *whoosh* tickled my ears when Darius shifted back, but I was too busy ridding myself of the bubble spell and digging his clothes out of my pack to watch this time. After handing over his pants, I grabbed a second pair for Quinn as he landed a few short feet away. Gaze lifted and cheeks red, I handed them over to the nude shifter before me.

"Thanks," he muttered, stuffing his slim yet taut legs into the black dress pants. "Any word from Catriona?"

"She'll be here," I assured him. "Give her time."

He shot me a quick look, almost as if he didn't believe me, then made his way over to his mother. I found the woman, the widow, wrapped in Darius's strong arms, her willowy, lean frame seeming frailer, more fragile than when we last met. It was concerning, given that it had only been a few weeks ago. She must have started mourning the loss of her husband before it even happened. I smoothed my hands down my sides without realizing it. My recovery from the djinn's poison had slimmed me down a little too, and I was eager for my curves back.

Mother and son eased apart, and my chest tightened at the sight of tears running down Cynthia's face, her cheeks on the verge of gaunt. Her husband's death had hit her hard—and rightly so. Arms wrapped around myself in a solo hug, I watched as Darius brushed his mother's stark white hair from her face— hair that tumbled down her back, thick and relatively straight. They said nothing to each other—at least, not out loud. I could only imagine what was said with nothing more than a look. After cupping Darius's scruffy cheeks one last time, her eyes twinkling, Cynthia moved on to Quinn.

While Quinn all but collapsed in his mother's arms, his shoulders shuddering and his sobs muffled against her, Darius had been the one to hold *her* up. In an instant, he had gone from son to protector, to support system, to an alpha without the title. I couldn't imagine how that would feel, to suddenly be the one a parent relied on for comfort when it had always been the other way around. Swallowing hard, I carefully picked my way across the stone path, giving him a moment to greet a somber Hayden with another strong, silent embrace.

Only when the youngest of the Thomas boys had moved over to Quinn and Cynthia did I run a hand over Darius's back. For just a moment, he seemed to relax under my touch. His shoulders rolled forward slightly, his jaw unclenched. I rubbed up and down over his heated skin, still coated in a fine layer of perspiration from the flight. The hint of nail across his shoulders seemed to rouse him, and with a hard blink, he stepped out of my reach. I could have taken it as a rejection, naturally, but the very idea of that faded when he pressed a quick kiss to my cheek and met my eyes with his steely gaze.

"I'm here," I whispered, "for whatever. Together, or not at all."

He nodded, his eyes saying our expression back to me before he turned and marched toward the alpha's hall with its dark windows and low-hanging banners.

"Kaye, sweet thing," Cynthia called while my eyes were momentarily fixed to Darius's retreating figure. Clearing my throat, I faced the approaching shifter with a sad smile, allowing myself to be enveloped in a gentle hug.

"I'm so sorry for your loss," I offered. No one wanted to hear it, but we all had to say it at some point. Her breath hitched briefly before she murmured her thanks in a voice barely breaking whisper volume. I patted her back, noting the thick brocade fabric of her black gown did nothing to hide her protruding bones. I needed to speak to Darius about this immediately. Grief could consume people if they weren't careful.

"Thank you for coming," Cynthia said after kissing me once on each cheek. "He will need your support now more than ever, I suspect. Past or future."

"I'm here to give it," I told her, wrapping an arm around her waist as we started our own slow march toward the alpha's hall. "For all of you, of course."

Hayden and I exchanged a quick greeting over his mother's shoulder, nothing more than a few eyebrow lifts and half smiles. The youngest Thomas son had always been so vibrant, so raring to go no matter the situation. To see him with the wind drudged out of his sails—devastating.

"We'll have the funeral tomorrow," Cynthia said, her voice distant. "I would have liked to hold off, keep Khalon for longer, but... the alpha ceremony, we need to..."

"I'm sure Khalon would understand," I offered, feeling as though I was propping her upright by the waist. "He knew his clan needs a leader."

"I don't know how I'm going to..." She blinked rapidly, as though only just realizing what she was admitting to me. A soft clearing of her throat followed, and then, "Do it. I don't know how I'm going to..."

"One step at a time," I said gently. Ahead, Darius stood with his head bowed, a hand resting on the door to what had once been his father's hall. I lifted my chin, determined to keep my cool, to be the backbone and strength that this family needed. "That's all anyone can ever do. Take it one step at a time, piece by piece, until it doesn't seem so frightening anymore..."

"I can do that," Cynthia murmured, and I caught her eye, smiling.

"I know you can. You won't be doing it alone, either."

None of them would. Not if I had anything to say about it.

THE LAST FUNERAL I HAD ATTENDED WAS A NON-MAGICAL, non-supernatural, non-*anything* affair in New York. One of our practice's patients had taken his own life, despite our best efforts to keep him on track with his depression treatment. While my partner kept the office running that day, I had gone as a representative for both of us. Swathed in my usual black and a hat with bird cage netting disguising my face from the few members of his family that showed, I was the one to pay tribute. The whole thing had been a quiet, somber ordeal. Nine people, myself included, showed for the service, and fewer stayed to watch the coffin lowered into the earth. I'd left feeling drained, both in body and spirit.

The funeral for Khalon Thomas was a different sort of thing *entirely*. Not only was the entire clan in attendance—having filled his old hall with flowers and trinkets, tokens of affection piled high wherever I looked—but the sheer volume of supernatural beings present, boggled my mind. Half of Alfheim must have been in attendance too, despite Khalon's hesitancy to work with supernaturals during the course of his life.

Apparently, his reputation warranted their attendance. Our bear shifter friends Colton and Liam arrived on behalf of their clan, their usual joker personas kept in check. Zayne sent Galen in his place, along with his apologies for being unable to tear himself away from Alfheim. I passed his words along to Darius and his family, but I figured my presence was enough representation for my family.

Not so, however. Early that morning, before the funeral proceedings began, before the sun crept even halfway above the horizon, my father and his children arrived with a band of Brisbane dragons in tow. They brought gifts for Cynthia and her sons: food, weapons, gold, silks. Hayden later explained to me the more opulent the funeral offerings, the more respected the alpha. While the Sanctius clan had gifted the Thomas family with mountains of treasures, nothing shone as brightly as what James Holloway offered before the proceedings began. I'd yet to see Cynthia cry today, but when she saw my father's gifts, she finally broke down, far from the eyes of her clan, and needed a lot of consoling from Darius before the floodgates closed.

Given what the day entailed, it certainly didn't surprise me that I'd barely seen Darius. We spent the night before in his old bedroom, but he was unable to sleep. Every couple of hours or so, I woke to see him staring out the window, hands clasped behind his back and jaw clenched. Since then, he'd been so busy with the funeral, with organizing and thanking all the attendees personally, that I counted myself lucky if I caught a full glimpse of him before the crowd swallowed him again.

At least, all that distance meant I got to spend more time with my newly acquired father and siblings. Catriona hung around too, in the same boat with Quinn as I was with Darius. She seemed to click with Hudson well; apparently my fae bestie was a magnet for the quieter, shyer men of the group. My new half-brother, however, never looked at Catriona like Quinn did, just as her gaze always seemed to drift in the middle Thomas son's direction whenever she had an idle moment.

It was a distraction I understood well.

After offerings were made at the alpha's hall, the family brought out the body of the fallen dragon king on a thick wooden pallet. Local flowers adorned the wooden pyre, and the Thomas boys—plus a cousin whose name I'd forgotten—each carried a corner of it on their shoulders.

"We're to follow them," James whispered quickly in my ear before ushering me toward the procession. We fell in line behind Cynthia, who followed her sons with a black veil hiding her face and her bony hands clutched together in front of her. Leda, Hudson and Catriona took their place behind us. Slowly the rest of the funeral-goers joined the line.

"Where are we going?" I asked. "Isn't there a service?"

"You just saw it," James told me as we marched in tandem. "The gift giving is in shifter tradition... It takes the place of speeches and such that you might see at human funerals."

"Oh." I glanced back at the alpha's hall with its doors flung open, a wreath of black roses hanging on each. "Right."

While it felt as though everything was happening at lightning speed, in reality we had been milling around the alpha's hall all morning as visitors arrived to pay their respects. Almost three hours had passed in the blink of an eye. I couldn't begin to imagine how exhausted my dragon must have felt.

We followed a well-worn path for some time. Drums now echoed from the clan section of the funeral march. Like the heartbeat of the group, the music set our pace, set our tone, kept our movements as one when we left the relatively even terrain for the unforgiving raw natural landscape of the mountain. Slowly, we crossed the entire range, coming to a cliff at the far end. A narrow plateau jutted out, upon which sat an already constructed pile of wood arranged like a bonfire. I swallowed hard, realizing there would be no burial for Khalon Thomas. His sons set his body upon the wood, dressed in nothing more than a cotton shift, with coins on his eyes and the fruits of the land by his side.

With a quick glance back, I frowned. While we had a clear view of what was going to happen, the clan and anyone beyond the first, perhaps, eight rows of people wouldn't be able to see anything. And I wondered, with a furtive look to my father, if that was the point—if we were arranged in order of importance. James was the alpha of a very powerful dragon clan. He had earned a spot behind the widow, his children behind him, but why was I so close?

My gaze darted to Darius, to his stony expression, to his set jaw and his clenched fist.

I was here because of him.

My dragon turned and marched back toward us, and Leda tugged me to one side as he passed through the crowd. I shot my half-sister a furrowed look, but she said nothing until, moments later, when Darius stalked back with a torch of flickering blue flame in hand.

"It's Darius's flame," Leda whispered as the crowd closed in again. "It's symbolic... The flame of the new alpha will take the soul of the old off to the otherworld."

"Plus," James cut in, "an alpha's flame is the only flame hot enough to truly incinerate a dragon shifter's remains and trigger the transformation."

"Transformation?" *Didn't incinerated mean burned to ash?*

. . .

"WHEN A DRAGON SHIFTER DIES, IT REVERTS TO HUMAN FORM. The heat of an alpha's flame is the only fire hot enough to burn a body designed to withstand high temperatures and allow the skull to reshape into dragon form."

I looked at him in astonishment. "How is that possible?"

"Kaye, my half fae, half dragon daughter, are you really asking me how anything is possible?"

I chuckled. "I guess not."

"The exact mechanism or magic of it, isn't really understood. We just know that only an alpha's fire can do it. And once the fire has consumed all of the body, burning away the human and dragon parts, when the flame finally dies out, the dragon skull will be all that remains—refined by fire."

"The fire will burn all night. In the morning, when it has died, the clan elder will remove the skull and take it to the sacred place," Leda explained. I bit my lip, wishing I'd known the lore already—wishing that this wasn't all a huge learning curve for me. Not because I felt left out, but I figured I could be a better support to Darius if I actually knew what was going on.

Standing before the pyre, Darius seemed to take a moment for himself, his head bowed and his eyes closed. Behind me, silence reigned over all those in attendance, the only sound was that of the fluttering clan banners, family flags, and the unforgiving wind. When the moment passed, my dragon tossed the torch onto his father's body. Moments later, the funeral pyre ignited, quickly engulfed by the searing blue flame. The flowers wilted to ash within seconds. The wood caught fire quickly. The body burned—without a smell, strangely enough. We all watched as the fire consumed Khalon Thomas. As I followed the smoke when it lifted away, catching on the wind, I had to wonder if there was any real stock in Leda's explanation of the spiritual significance of the ceremony.

But the debate over whether we had souls and if there was an afterlife—it was too grand a topic for me to dwell on. Instead, I focused my mind, clearing it of everything but the passing moments, and watched until the flame reduced Darius's father to a pile of dust. It was then that Cynthia stepped forward and reached into the fire, retracting her hand quickly with a hiss.

"The ash of the old alpha," my father murmured. "Darius will wear it until his own alpha ceremony tomorrow."

Cynthia smeared the black powder across Darius's forehead, then stepped back and pressed that same hand to her heart. The fire continued to burn, but as the Thomas family made their way back toward the crowd, I assumed we weren't going to stay and watch it die. I stepped aside, Leda and I on one side, my father, Hudson, and Catriona on the other, and bowed my head slightly as the family passed. When I lifted my gaze, I spied mourners reaching out to touch Darius as he marched through. Not once did he stop, though he did glance back, his stormy eyes searching me out. This time, I didn't smile. I just nodded.

I wasn't going anywhere.

"And now," James said with a sigh, "we eat. Kaye?"

His hand on my back roused me into motion. The crowd closed ahead of us, effectively making us the last in line.

"We eat?" I said, processing it more slowly than I should have as we started to walk.

"A *lot*," Hudson told me. "We eat a *lot*."

"Good." Catriona placed a hand on her stomach. "I'm starving." Her eyes widened suddenly as her cheeks flushed. "Oh. Was that inappropriate? I just—"

"I can hear your stomach from here," I teased, hoping to alleviate any impending panic as I linked arms with her. "Come on. I'm sure there's something that'll sustain you."

Given how grand the funeral had been already, I couldn't fathom the spread the clan would have to honor Khalon one last time. My stomach gurgled at the thought.

But before I could satisfy it, I had to find Darius. This distance, this separation, had gone on long enough. I didn't care if it was against protocol. I didn't care if there were other people who wanted to speak with him first. As soon as we returned to the alpha's hall, my dragon would become mine again—and if anyone wanted to say something about it, I welcomed the challenge.

He might be the clan's alpha-to-be, but first and foremost, he was my dragon.

And nothing was going to change that.

$\maltese$ 2 $\maltese$

JAMES AND HUDSON WAS RIGHT—I'D never seen so much food in one place in all my life. Roasts as far as the eye could see. Mountains of mashed potatoes paired with dark leafy greens. Whole birds of every variety: turkey, chicken, pheasant, duck, raven. Fish, both raw and cooked. Even the pickiest of eaters could find something sumptuous and delicious at Khalon Thomas's funeral feast, though that wasn't the reason my mood had improved. Once we had all arrived back at the alpha's hall, seating was assigned, and for the first time all day, I was placed directly at Darius's side—and there I had been for the last hour.

Just like the first feast I'd experienced with the Sanctius clan, I sat sandwiched between Darius and Hayden. Khalon's seat remained empty, and Quinn spent much of the meal thus far, prompting his mother to finish her plate. Darius, meanwhile, hadn't touched much of anything, though he'd pushed everything around into a pile of goopy, green-brown mush.

Catriona was granted a seat at the head table next to Quinn, which was the only change to the seating assignments from my last meal here. The Brisbane clan, with James and my step-siblings closest to the head of the hall, occupied the table my supernatural militia once had. The Sanctius clan took up the other long tables. Supernaturals of all kinds were interspersed between the shifters. Their innate magical pulse paired with the roar of the diners gave me a bit of a headache.

Still, even the slight twinge behind my right eye couldn't upset me. After all, there were at least a hundred people seated outside, and even more trickling down into the village below. It could have been much, much worse.

What *did* upset me, just a little, was the general sense of unease I'd had since I sat down. My inner voice had been relatively silent all day, perhaps in deference to the fallen alpha, but now she wouldn't shut up, insisting I look here, there and everywhere to find the source of my discomfort. It was that feeling—like I was being watched? I couldn't shake it. Never mind the fact that I knew I *was* being watched. Seated beside Darius, I was sure the eyes of every shifter and supernatural present had darted in my direction at least once since the feast began. However, the gaze that sent the hairs on the back of my neck up, that encouraged a bout of gooseflesh across my arms, hadn't diverted. It had stayed, fixed, and wouldn't let up.

At least, that was my working theory. If I couldn't shake the feeling, there had to be *some* merit to it. Still, I did what I could to distract myself with the thousand other things going on around me. All throughout the meal, visitors approached Darius to offer whispered sympathies and subtle congratulations about his upcoming ascension to the Sanctius throne. When the most recent one shuffled back to his seat, I set my hand on Darius's forearm, smiling softly when his weary gaze slowly turned to me.

"Hey." I gave a little squeeze. "You doing okay?"

"Been better."

"I believe that." His world was in the process of spinning upside-down. Of course, he'd been better. Still, there was a tightness in his mouth area, one I'd noticed since we sat down, that was tough to ignore. "Anything in particular being especially bothersome?"

"My uncle should be here," he said tightly, his voice lowering.

In my peripheral, I caught Hayden glance our way, but he said nothing, glumly stabbing at his pile of buttery mashed potatoes instead.

"Uncle?"

"My father's brother, Kain," Darius told me, his scowl prominent. "He rules another clan, and he, of all these people, should be here right now. If not for my father, then for my mother. They've always been good friends."

"Maybe…" I pressed my lips together with a soft clearing of my throat. No. Offering the classic *maybe something came up* wouldn't do much to soothe Darius's warranted irritation. "We'll deal with it later. Try not to let it get you down."

"Ah, yes, I suppose there *are* a few more pressing issues to bum me out at my father's funeral than my uncle flaking."

I tensed, expecting his glare to fix directly on me, but he wore a bit of a half-grin instead. Nothing like his usual handsome smile, but it was enough to let me know my dragon was still in there. Somewhere. Buried deep, at least for the time being.

Just as I was about to ask Darius the nature of his father and uncle's relationship—maybe they weren't as close as Darius assumed—another mourner strode up to the head table, making a beeline for Darius. While normally I turned away and let Darius have his moment with the well-wisher, this time I couldn't. As the man approached, I couldn't get a clear reading on his supernatural background—which concerned me more than I cared to admit. There was a whiff of a combination, perhaps, yet it remained muddled in my mind's eye. Supernatural, definitely. Shifter—maybe? There were so many different creatures in the hall that it was like their essences overwhelmed my ability to read people.

Tall, lean and moderately attractive, he wore all black, his trench coat fluttering dramatically behind him. Thick black facial hair coated his cheeks, leading up to a pair of startlingly bright, blue eyes. Cold. Distant. Like an underweight Siberian husky.

Kind of like Jasmine, actually. I bit the insides of my cheeks, not wanting to put my immense dislike for the fae onto a stranger who, for all I knew, could have been the nicest man in the world.

"My condolences, Darius Thomas," the man said, his voice a rumbly roughness with a faint hint of nasal. I grabbed my drink and took a quick sip. What an odd combination, just like his supernatural background. Trying not to overtly stare, I eyeballed him a few seconds longer, trying to get a read—and failing.

"Thank you." Darius shook the man's extended hand. "Did you know my father?"

"In an age gone by," the man remarked, holding Darius's gaze, lips quirked in a slight smirk. "Hector. I assisted with some permit issues in Alfheim from time to time. When I'd heard that he passed, I knew I had to show my face. He was a good man. A good alpha."

"I appreciate the sentiment," Darius said, and I caught the way his gaze flicked to his mother and back again. "Kind words go far today."

"Of course." Hector retracted his hand, his knuckles white— as though he'd been squeezing harder than necessary. *Curious.* "I've heard many kind words about you today as well. I'm sure your father would be proud to have you fill his shoes." Then, that icy blue stare slid over to me. "And your mate. I've heard nothing but positivity around the famous Kaye Allister. Truly impressive. A hybrid, is she not?"

"She is," I answered briskly, annoyed that he spoke about me like I wasn't there. Darius sat up a little straighter, as if sensing my anger. However, before either of us could get another word in, Hector dipped his head and stepped back.

"I didn't mean to offend." He looked to Darius. "Again. My deepest sympathies, but I know the Sanctius clan is in excellent hands. Thank you for your time."

And with that, he disappeared into the hall, his black attire soon blending with the sea of mourners in similar garb. I sat back with a huff. *Rude jerk.*

"Ignore him," Darius muttered, picking at the turkey drumstick on his plate, the only thing spared from his pile of mush. I watched him strip the meat off, then set it down without eating it. "How have you been with your father here? Any problems?"

"No, he's been fantastic," I noted, my eyes darting to the Brisbane clan table briefly. "All three of them have been great, actually."

"Good. I invited them to stay for the alpha ceremony tomorrow, but if you wanted them gone, I could rescind the invitation."

"Wouldn't that be, like, political suicide?"

He shrugged, his lips lifted in that half-grin again. "A bit."

"Well, thank you for inviting them." They had been so helpful explaining the nuances of the alpha's funeral today; I imagined I'd need the same sort of support tomorrow, as no one had told me what to expect yet.

From the look on Darius's face, however, he knew *exactly* what to expect—and didn't seem too pleased about it. I placed a hand on his arm again, and just as I tried to steer the conversation somewhere lighter, somewhere more pleasant, a new trio of mourners wandered up to the table to speak with him.

Instantly, I lost him to the clan, but made a note that sometime later, I'd make him smile again. A real smile. One that would reach his eyes and warm my heart.

"Sorry, Kaye, we haven't seen Darius," Catriona told me, her head to tipped to one side, her hands full of funeral trinkets. "Last I saw, he was with you."

"Yeah, I know. We seem to have gotten separated." I ran a hand through my hair, finally letting it free from the restrictive braid crown Catriona had weaved it into early that morning.

Thinking back to that moment when she put the final pin in place—it felt like an eternity ago. It was hard to believe so much had happened in a single day.

The feast had lasted for hours, well into the night. With food and wine provided from visiting clans and the Sanctius storerooms alike, the eating, drinking, toasting, laughing, *crying* went on forever. By the time the final guests departed, both local dragons and visitors alike, I wanted to collapse into a ball on the floor and sleep well into next week. However, there was still *so* much to do before any of us could turn in. Since my father was staying to witness the alpha ceremony tomorrow, he took control of the few Brisbane dragons who stayed behind to help with the clean-up. Leda and Hudson were on garbage patrol outside, collecting discarded plates and wrappers and whatever else people had seen fit to throw around the drunker they got. Quinn and Catriona picked through the gifts, sorting them all into keep and donate piles, and Hayden was tasked with putting Cynthia to bed.

While the woman hadn't drunk an excessive amount of wine, she also hadn't touched a bite of her food. The alcohol had hit her hard and fast toward the end of the funeral festivities, and the fact that everyone else was a bit cheery thanks to the booze, certainly wasn't helping her mental state. Darius had ushered her out before he gave his thank-you-for-coming speech, but now Hayden had to make sure Cynthia actually stayed in bed. No one wanted to go searching the mountain at night for a drunk, devastated woman who probably wouldn't want to be found.

As for me, I tried to help out wherever I could. I escorted tipsy supernaturals to a few temporary portals at the base of the mountain. I enchanted the stone sinks in the kitchens to act as magical dishwashers—because if they had to wash all these plates by hand, they'd still be doing it a year from now. I picked up garbage outside with Leda and Hudson, I spoke for Darius in his absence when clan members came looking, and I loaded

Hayden up with soft blankets and some herbal tea to take to his mother.

But all I wanted to do, however, was speak to Darius—alone. And now he was gone. Without a trace. Lips pursed, I thanked my best friend quickly, nodded to a sullen, exhausted Quinn, then made my way out of the dark, smelly alpha's hall and into the night air. As refreshing as it was, I wouldn't breathe easily until I found him. After checking his old bedroom, his mother's room, *and* a few of the mountaintop sites he had been especially vocal about the first time I toured the village, I found nothing.

Not wanting to go back to work without giving it my all, I headed as far from the noise and hubbub of the clean-up crew as I could. Then, in the quiet, I closed my eyes, breathed deeply, and told my inner voice to shut up for two seconds so I could listen to my gut instead. She complied, though only just, the whispers caressing the fringes of my mind, encouraging me to find him, to go to him, to comfort him.

"What do you think I'm trying to do here?" I snapped, glaring up at my forehead. Squaring my shoulders, I stared out into the night, lifting my gaze up to the starry, clear sky—wondering if I might find him there.

I didn't. There were no dragon cries on the wind. No thundering flaps of his wings.

Knowing that he had to be here *somewhere*, that Darius wasn't the type to throw his hands up and bail when things got tough, I just started walking. With no set path in mind and no particular route to follow, I let my feet steer me. I wasn't one for meditation, but I managed to clear my mind just enough so that persistent thoughts, good or bad, wouldn't cloud my feet's judgement. I wanted to let them do their thing. Because with every step, something inside me told me I was following in Darius's footsteps, that even though I couldn't see the evidence, this was the path he had walked sometime earlier.

Sure enough, my feet led me down the mountain, away from the village halls and off the beaten path. The air warmed the closer to the ground I walked, until finally I was at the foot of one mountain in the range, my legs tired and my eyes heavy.

But at least my feet had stepped up to the plate and done their job. Because there was Darius, some twenty feet away, seated at the edge of a lake so dark, I could have sworn the water was black. He stopped skipping stones as I made my way over, though he didn't turn back, not even when I smoothed a hand over his hunched shoulder.

"Hey."

"Hey," he muttered, his voice hoarse. He looked down at the stone in his hand. Smooth. Oval. He turned it over and over, before rearing back and hurling it toward the water. Rather than skipping as the others had, it landed with a heavy *plunk* and disappeared. Nibbling my lower lip, I eased around to the other side of him, then perched on what looked like a recently fallen tree trunk. When he didn't immediately lean into me, I wondered if he needed the space—then shook my head and shuffled closer until he had his arm around me. I locked myself around his waist, with my head resting on his shoulder, and listened to the slow, steady beat of his heart, to the blood pumping through his veins.

"How are you doing?" I murmured.

"Fine," he answered without pause, without hesitation, his words thick—restrained. I could feel the control radiating through him, his body stiff and his jaw clenched. He wasn't fine. Darius was far from fine, but I knew pushing too hard could backfire. So, I softened my tone, set my hand on his thick thigh, and sighed.

"You know... It's okay *not* to be fine, too," I told him. "No one else has to know. It's just me and you."

"I have to be fine, Kaye," he said with a slight shake of his head. "Tomorrow I become the clan alpha. I can't be..."

"Sad?"

"I have to be strong," he growled, then untangled himself from my grasp and stood. I watched him pace the edge of the lake for a few moments, his hands swinging in tight fists by his sides. "There's no weakness in alphas. Our dragons don't respect weakness. They pounce. They exploit. They purge it from their homes. I can't..."

"You aren't weak to mourn the death of your father," I argued. He stopped, kicking up a bit of wet rock and dirt as he did. Although he didn't face me, I caught the quiver in his lower lip, the faraway look in his eyes as he studied the dark lake. Slowly, without the constant assault of his rocks, the water settled to a stillness, save for the flutter of fish beneath its surface.

"I..." Darius planted his hands on his hips, his head bowed and his eyes closed. "I don't think I can do this, Kaye."

I cautiously stood and joined him at the edge of the lake. While I wanted to touch him, to drag him into my arms and brush my fingers through his hair, it wasn't what *he* wanted. In a moment of perceived weakness, no one wanted to be physically coddled—as if he *was* weak.

"What do you mean?" I tipped my head to one side, frowning at him. "You don't think you can become alpha? Pretty sure it's a done deal—"

"I don't think I can fill his shoes," he insisted. "I don't think I can handle the responsibility of taking care of all these people, shifters I've known my entire life. All of them will look at me now to fix everything. Their lives are in my hands, and I don't think I deserve such a huge responsibility. I mean, *what* have I done to warrant any of this? Just because I was *born,* doesn't mean I deserve to take his place."

I bit my lip, waiting a few beats in case he needed to keep ranting. Then, with a soft sigh, I touched his bicep and found it tense beneath my fingers.

"Darius, you weren't just *born*. You were born to do this. Everyone knows it. They can all sense it."

"But—"

"If you weren't ready, your father wouldn't have left you alone to do it," I told him, raising my voice to drown him out for a moment. "Seriously. He had faith in you. Not only that, but *I* have faith in you. I've watched you display leadership and sacrifice. I've seen you defeat magical beings with powers far greater than your own, and I've watched you protect the weak. Sure, I don't know much about this alpha business, but to me, you have exemplified over and over again the true qualities of a leader. You *can* do this. I know you can. You *will* do this, because that's the kind of person you are."

I sucked in a much-needed gasp when I finished; apparently, I'd been rambling on a lot longer than I realized, judging by the slightly wide-eyed expression on Darius's face. Hands limp at his side, he stared at me, capturing my gaze with his stormy grays, and I suddenly found myself anxious for a response. *Had I overstepped my bounds? Was that not what he wanted, or needed, to hear —at all?*

"Darius, I didn't mean to overstep—"

He silenced me with a kiss, leaning down and scooping me up with an arm around my waist, his lips capturing mine in a heated embrace. I felt the moment flood my body, a rush of excitement paired with a spark of longing burning brightly within my core. Exhaling sharply, I threaded my fingers up through his hair, smiling against his mouth at the rumbling growl reverberating in his chest when I tugged twice for good measure. The sound penetrated through me, shooting straight to the crux of my thighs, the longing unfurling into something akin to dark desire—to desperate need.

Much to my disappointment, Darius pulled back as soon as the kiss threatened to deepen, nipping lightly at my lower lip before he straightened.

"You didn't overstep," he murmured, his words colored with a rasp that made my toes curl. "You never do, Kaye. You always know just what to say to pull me back from the edge."

My hands slid down his neck to rest on his burly shoulders, and I flicked my hair back, smirking.

"What can I say... It's like knowing what to do in a mental crisis is my job, or something."

At the very least, it *had* been my job. I hadn't practiced psychology professionally in months. Maybe that was why I was so on the ball with everybody's feelings today—therapist withdrawal.

"Either way, thank you." He stole another quick peck when I didn't expect it. While the starlight illuminated our surroundings, I hoped it was still dark enough that he couldn't spot my blush.

"So, shall we head back?" I asked, nodding toward the mountains looming behind us. "Or do you want to stay here for a bit?"

"Let's go," he said, looking just as reluctant to fully untangle as I felt. "I'm sure there's still a lot to do."

"You know how many gifts there are to sort through? It's insane."

"It's a compliment."

"One well earned, I think." We exchanged smiles before turning away from the lake, hand in hand, and strolled toward the unseen trail I'd taken down here at a good clip. As we walked, however, something washed over me—like a summer's breeze, but cold. A flash of adrenaline pumped from the top of my head straight down to my toes, firing up everything in between. My fight or flight instinct kicked into high gear seemingly out of nowhere. I whirled around.

"Kaye?" Darius stopped as I scanned the area. Nothing but forest and underbrush and the lake out here. In the distance, an owl hooted.

"I thought I felt... something," I said, frowning. "But it must have just been the wind." I looked up at him. "Are you cold?"

Darius shrugged. "No, but I kind of always burn hot."

"True." Heart hammering, I took one last look before calling it. Clearly Darius wasn't the only one reeling from a stressful, *long* day. Apparently, I was just jittery...

Though as we started our climb, hands clasped, the hairs on

the back of my neck slowly rose, and once again, I felt an unflinching stare fixated on my back.

Yet when I glanced over my shoulder, I saw nothing.

But the feeling of being watched...

Those eyes.

Not once, for the whole climb, did they ever blink.

3

"Hey," Leda nudged me with her elbow, "you promise, you're going to keep it together?"

"What, for more speeches? I think I can manage," I whispered back, eyes fixed on Darius, Cynthia, and some decrepit shifter I'd come to learn was the village elder. Apparently the oldest in the clan, along with the spouse of the fallen alpha, led the ceremony that transferred Khalon's responsibilities to his son. For the last hour, as we all stood watching in an enormous semi-circle in front of the alpha's hall, there had been a lot of talking, walking around a bonfire holding hands, and ceremonial throat singing from the elder. I wasn't sure what I'd expected when it came to an alpha ceremony, but probably not this.

At least the mood had lifted from yesterday. And, why shouldn't it? This was a joyous moment for the Sanctius clan. Although there were only a few supernatural beings present, the air hummed with magic—magic I could only assume stemmed from the clan's excitement at the crowning of their new king. While most of the flags and banners still hung low in deference to Darius's father, some were up and flying high already. Quinn told Catriona and I that everyone would raise new banners and new flags once the alpha ceremony was completed. Then there would be feasting, dancing, and general merriment well into the night.

Another exhausting day, but at least I had seen Cynthia smile —and eat.

"No, what's next isn't a speech," Leda told me. I stood sandwiched between her and my father, hands clasped in front of me, dressed in a crimson gown that Cynthia had worn when Khalon was sworn in. The damn thing was so tight that I worried I'd split it right down the sides of I took too deep of a breath, but I appreciated the gesture—even if it was woefully inappropriate for such a scorching, hot summer day. On top of that, I missed my trademark black attire, even if Darius couldn't take his eyes off my butt earlier.

"More awkward singing?" I didn't want to knock an ancient tradition, something that had kept Darius up most of last night —something that was such a huge deal to him. But I was tired. My patience was a little lower today. My feet hurt from standing in one place for so long. I adored my dragon, but just put the freakin' crown on his head already. He needed for this to be over —and I seriously wanted it for be over *for* him. The stress of a parent's funeral one day, and then *this* the next? Brutal.

"No..." Leda pressed her lips together when our father shot us a pointed look. I bit the insides of my cheeks, trying not to smile as my half-sister and I exchanged side-long glances. Shifting my weight from side to side, I straightened somewhat at the sight of Cynthia and the clan elder disappearing inside the alpha's hall. Darius stood before the small bonfire, hands hovering over it.

"Where did they go?" I murmured, trying not to move my lips much. "Is it over?"

Leda shook her head. "Not quite."

Frowning, I watched as Cynthia and the elder returned, each carrying a torch. The elder carried one with a blue flame, which I instantly noted belonged to Darius. I'd recognize it anywhere. The other burned a breathtaking red—pure and stark against the gray backdrop of the mountains. In fact, it looked a little like the color of my dress. I twisted my hands together, anxiety prickling through me.

"What are those for?"

"*Promise* you'll keep it together?"

"Leda."

"Kaye, promise—"

"Both of you," James hissed, still facing the ceremony, "be *silent*."

My mouth opened in protest, but then quickly shut again when Darius stepped around the bonfire and held his arms out. Palms twisted toward the sky, he met my gaze briefly before closing his eyes and tilting his head back.

"What...?" My sassy inquiries died on the tip of my tongue when both Cynthia and the elder *lit each of Darius's arms on fire*. A strangled screech slipped out of me as the blue and red flames spread across his bland cotton shirt, colliding on his chest and engulfing his body. Panicked, I lunged forward, hands pulsing with magic, ready to extinguish the flames, but both Leda and James dragged me back.

"He's fine," James assured me. "It's all part of the ceremony."

"He's on *fire*," I snapped. "He can't be *fine*!"

"Dragons live in fire," Leda countered, her grip tightening on my arm when I tried to wriggle free. "Seriously. He's okay."

I faced him, my breath coming hard and fast, unable to feel my toes, and watched as the fire consumed him. For a moment, the flames retained their separate colors—until finally they merged, blending into a beautiful, soothing purple, the heat of which washed over me some twenty feet away.

"The flame of the old," Cynthia cried, her voice echoing across the mountaintop.

"The flame of the new," the elder chimed in.

In unison, they said: "Darius Thomas is reborn... alpha."

The purple flame disappeared, as if absorbed by his skin, leaving him naked but unburned. The elder strode forth and threw a shawl over Darius's broad shoulders, which he used to cover himself as the crowd around me broke out into thundering cheers.

"No one could have warned me he was going to be lit on fire?!" I demanded, a sickly feeling creeping up my body, unleashing some unholy combination that made me feel as though I was about to vomit *and* faint.

"Everyone should experience the surprise of an alpha ceremony, at least once," James said, grinning. "What takes place isn't discussed *ever*. If you are fortunate enough to witness it, then—"

He hastily caught my other arm when my knees buckled. Moments later, Darius was by my side, smiling broadly for the first time in days.

"Are you all right?" he asked, smoothing a hand over my face, tucking my hair behind my ear. "I'm sure that was a bit frightening, but—"

"A bit frightening?!" I quickly found my footing, wrenched myself free from Leda and James, and pushed at Darius's chest with all my might. "Are you *kidding* me?!"

"Kaye—"

"I'm just so..." With shaking, clammy hands, I threw my arms around him, still torn between pushing him again and kissing him in front of everyone. In the end, I let go of my shock, my surprise, and my near heart attack, and instead whispered in his ear, "I'm so proud of you."

"Thank you," he rumbled back, squeezing me softly before stepping away, his hands on my shoulders. "I'm sorry I couldn't give you a heads up. For the record, I'd react the exact same way if someone set you on fire."

"And I'm sure you'd be justified," I told him. I, on the other hand, kind of made a fool of myself in front of everyone by over-reacting, but at least no one could question just how much I loved my dragon.

"Darius, my darling!" Cynthia swept over and wrapped her

son in a brief embrace, her eyes shining with tears—but her smile outshining us all. "Your father would be so proud of you!"

Darius scratched at the back of his neck, clearly a little uneasy with all this attention. The clan still hadn't stopped cheering. "Thanks, Mom."

"Of course." She patted his cheek, then shot a quick glance back to me. "Now you just need to find yourself a mate and you'll be all set. I think I know the perfect candidate."

My cheeks darkened as all eyes in the nearby proximity darted to me. *Oi.* Nothing quite like a huge ceremony and everyone watching to put pressure on a relationship.

"I..." I swallowed hard, that about-to-faint-and-hurl feeling hitting me again—hard. "I think I need to sit down..."

Luckily for me, my bestie had my back. Catriona hurried forward, linked her arm with mine, and all but dragged me away, insisting I'd be back in a few minutes once the shock of the ceremony wore off.

But I wasn't coming back in a few minutes. I couldn't return to the stares, to the whispers, to the expectations.

Not yet. I needed time to think—alone—and I couldn't decide whether that made me selfish or practical. All I knew was that this was the first time in months that I felt like I could come up for air, to stop and consider the cluster-fuck of *everything* that had happened since I stumbled upon Darius in that cave on our fae sister retreat.

And I was going to take the time I needed, damn it. I owed myself that much.

THUNDER RUMBLED OVERHEAD, THE HEAT OF A SWELTERING mid-summer's day carrying on into the late evening. The clouds rolled in shortly after the alpha ceremony, and I watched them steadily darken for hours. From my spot overlooking the valley below, I experienced the air thicken, and with the telltale sound of thunder in the distance, I knew the humidity had finally broken. Seconds later, a trio of lightning bolts cracked across the sky, illuminating the nearly black storm clouds drifting my way with the evening wind.

I should've gone back. Only an idiot sat outside during a thunderstorm, but I hadn't been able to *think* yet. Earlier, I couldn't justify not returning for the festivities after the ceremony. Once I calmed down, I was back by Darius's side, smiling and laughing and taking in the open love and affection the clan had to offer. I should have felt *good* after, but with Cynthia dropping more little hints for hours, I left the alpha's hall as things were dying down more frazzled than ever.

I loved Darius—that much was clear. Honestly, I couldn't imagine spending a day apart, and it wasn't because we were in the honeymoon phase of an early relationship. This was *real*. It was earnest and true, and I wanted to give in wholeheartedly.

But did I want to be an alpha's mate? Not only did I have *no* idea what that entailed beyond popping out kids to further the bloodline, I wasn't sure I wanted to get married—period. I'd never been the girl who fawned over wedding gowns or planned the perfect ceremony. It just wasn't me. Things were fine the way they were now. Great, even. Why complicate it?

My ears twitched at the sound of footsteps approaching, and I didn't need to look back to figure out who it was.

"I was wondering where you'd wandered off to," Darius said as he perched next to me on the rock ledge overlooking the valley. "Storm's coming."

I nodded. "I've already seen the lightning."

Darius studied the clouds for a moment, then stood and took my hand. "Come on. I think we need to have a talk."

"Normally that phrase is the kiss of death for relationships," I told him as he helped me up. "You planning on dumping me?"

He smirked. "No. Are you?"

"Of course not." I didn't have to think twice about it. Just because I was scared of the future and all that it might entail, certainly didn't mean I wanted to run.

"Did my mom freak you out with all that mate talk earlier?"

I shrugged as I followed him along the uneven path I'd taken to get way out here, far from the clan's celebrations. "A bit."

"I figured," he said with a sigh. "So, I think we should talk about it."

I bit the insides of my cheeks to keep from smiling. If a guy actually wanted to *talk* about uncomfortable problems in the relationship, he was definitely a keeper.

"I could get on board with that."

"Good." He turned back, his head cocked to one side and a sumptuous grin on his lips—the kind I wanted to kiss. However, as he drew a breath, perhaps to tease more, the clouds finally opened. We both stopped as frigid rain hammered down from the sky, soaking us by the bucketful. There was no gentle warning mist, no hesitant sprinkling—the storm began with a wholehearted downpour. I couldn't wipe the surprise from my features as freezing water ate through my clothes and coated my skin. Within seconds, I was wet down to the bone.

Much to my delight, Darius wore an equally flabbergasted look, and the thin fabric of his plain white tee stuck to all the dips and rises of his muscular torso. My eyes wandered across his body, blinking hard to keep the rain at bay, and when I licked my lips, he snorted.

"Down girl," he teased, running a hand through his hair and pushing the wild mass of brown-blond locks back. My eyes jumped back to his, to those storm-cloud grays that always seemed to darken when we were truly alone, and I shook my head.

"No." I hurried forward, fisting my hands in the soaked material of his shirt and dragging him down for a kiss. He fell into me all too willingly, an arm locked around my waist as he hoisted me up. Heat pounded through me, growing fierier with every beat of my heart until it spread through my entire system. Our lips met and parted in an instant, his tongue sweeping into my mouth and stroking mine, coaxing it out to play as I moaned. Darius responded with a growl, marching me backward until I stumbled into a rocky alcove, its barely-there overhang offering a brief reprieve from the rain. My hands cupped his strong jaw, and my tentative whispers of arousal morphed into full-blown gales when he snatched my wrists and pinned them back against the rock.

In that moment, I wanted him to devour me—mind, body, and soul. All the issues I'd been mulling over as I watched the storm roll in, they didn't matter. Right then and there, it was just Darius and I, together, with the storm at our backs and the future ahead. I arched against him, moaning softly when he nibbled at my lower lip, then dragged his parted lips along my jaw and down to my neck. The flash of teeth across my skin—*oh* it made my toes curl and my body throb with need.

My little mewl of protest when he withdrew, however, brought a rush of heat to my cheeks, diverting it away from the other more exciting bits as I flushed.

"You're shivering," Darius said, his voice thick and raspy. He dropped my wrists and ran his hands over me as his mouth twisted in a seductive grin. "Is it me or the cold?"

I rolled my eyes, only then noticing the way my teeth chattered. "Full of yourself much?"

"Just as I suspected." He shook his head. "I've been known to have that effect on—"

A swift smack to his chest forced a laugh out of him rather than the clichéd line I knew was coming. We both smirked at one another, and while I would have preferred to stay out here forever, the moment, *our* moment, was being carried away on the howling winds. The temperatures had dropped so suddenly, the high humidity of the night finally disappearing and ushering in the gale.

"Come on," he muttered, threading his fingers around mine. "Let's get you inside before you freeze to death."

"Someone's a little melodramatic," I said with a snort. After one last shared look, we dashed out into the rain. Fat, heavy droplets pummeled me as we ran, and while I could have used a spell to keep us dry, I didn't want to. There was something terribly romantic about making a mad dash through a storm with the rain unrelenting and the lightning flashing. Every so often, Darius turned back and swept me into his arms, and our mouths met with all the fury of the crashing booms of thunder overhead. Then we'd pull apart, smiling or laughing or teasing one another, and start the run again. In the end, it took us twice as long to get back to his room as it should have.

Darius had yet to move into the alpha's hall, and we instead locked ourselves inside his old bedroom—nothing more than a single wood and stone hall with sleeping quarters and a bathroom. He got a fire going in the old hearth while I changed out of my wet clothes. Then we both crawled into his king-sized bed, tucking one another under the covers, our bodies entwined, as the storm howled outside, its wrath slamming against the windows.

"Kaye," he murmured, pressing a kiss to my temple, "about today..."

I swallowed hard, knowing exactly where this conversation was leading. "Yeah?"

"You know what it means," he said, "now that I'm alpha, don't you?"

"In theory," I told him honestly.

"It means no one will settle until I find a mate. My mother wasn't just teasing today. It's quite serious."

I closed my eyes at his words, listening to the gentle crackling of the fire on the other side of the room. Darius's fingers grazed up and down my back lazily, and while he might seem relaxed to an outsider, I could tell the conversation weighed just as heavily on him. "Oh," was the best I could do.

"If I had my way, I know exactly who I would choose," he insisted, pulling me closer against his naked torso as my heart skipped a beat. He didn't need to say it outright. Of course, I knew he meant me.

"When I think of a shifter's mate, I'm sorry, but I think of someone who is just there to pump out a bunch of kids and keep the family name going," I admitted, my tone soft. I didn't want to offend him, but I couldn't help the way I imagined it. "You know I'd never agree to that... You know I'd want to work *with* you. Fight with you."

"I wouldn't have it any other way," he assured me, and I let out a little sigh of relief. At least I hadn't upset him, *and* he wasn't gearing up to ask me to be his broodmare. It was a good start. "Besides, that's a bit of an antiquated idea about the role of a shifter's wife, *especially* an alpha's wife."

"Okay." I sat up, my hand resting on his chest, and met his eyes. "So, tell me straight up, what this would entail. If you want me to make an informed decision—"

"I do."

"Then I need to know all the facts." Thunder rattled the windows, followed swiftly by a bolt of lightning so bright that it illuminated the small hall like it was daylight. I gave the storm my attention for a few moments, then sighed. Darius's gaze had never left my face.

"Shifters mate for life. They're bound to one another," he told me quietly, taking my hand in his. "It's a very serious commitment that no one takes lightly."

"Good. Because neither do I." I had no interest in devoting myself to a man, to falling in love and making a vow, if it was a meaningless, casual affair.

Darius smiled, clearly pleased with my response. "The wives of alphas are not just there to produce the *next* alpha. You would be responsible for the clan in equal measures like I am. When I'm away, they're all yours. *You* are their queen, their mother, and their keeper." I gulped, the gravity of the situation making my stomach turn. "To be an alpha wife is to be a leader. Agreeing to be my mate... It isn't just a matter of getting married and living happily ever after. It's a commitment. It's a promise to give yourself wholeheartedly to the clan in the same way you give yourself to your mate. It's a job and title that's just as important as mine."

He brushed my wet hair from my face, sweeping it back behind my ears. The caress of his skin against mine sent a shiver racing through my body, and in an instant, it quieted my racing mind.

"I love you, Kaye, my fae," he told me, and my whole body prickled with emotion. *I love you.* We'd never said it to each other. Before I could stop them, tears pooled and threatened to fall, but I blinked them back as Darius added, "But I would never force this life on you. I want you to know how much work and responsibility the position requires, because I want you to be happy. I would understand if you... said no."

I looked back out the window. The storm had quieted somewhat, perhaps having blown over the mountains, but rain continued to drizzle down the glass panes. Being an alpha's mate, fated or not, carried a huge responsibility with it. Was that why my mom left James? Could she not handle the responsibilities? If her love for him was even a fraction of what I felt for Darius, it must have broken her heart to walk away from him. How it must have broken his too. Now that I knew all that was required of an alpha's wife, I had a lot to consider—and it wasn't an answer I could give tonight.

So, I responded to what I knew with certainty.

"I love you too, Darius Thomas," I said, my lips mirroring the enormous smile that spread across his face. "I'll have to think about this. If it was as simple as saying yes to a normal proposal, I'm pretty sure I know the answer already."

"Well," his fingers walked up my arm and clutched at my chin, drawing me toward him, "that says something."

"But I need to think," I repeated, happily nuzzling against his chest, my arms snaking around his neck. "I'm not sure I'm ready for the life you just described, as much as I love you."

"Mmm keep saying it," he purred, tipping my head back and

stealing a quick kiss. I all but melted into him, my eyes fluttering closed until he pulled back slightly. "I hope you remember that I'm not someone who takes no for an answer very well. I'll pursue you. I've done it before. I have no problems doing it again."

"I welcome the chase." And I meant it. I needed to know that this was what *he* wanted too, after all.

"You'll get it in spades."

I grinned and kissed his stubbly cheek, then settled down against him. As his hand slowly worked into my hair, massaging my scalp in slow, even strokes, I watched the fire flicker in the hearth. Hypnotic, comforting, the dance of the flames and the rhythmic fall of the rain lulled me to sleep. My thoughts, my fears, my concerns—I tucked them away. For now, I basked in the warmth of Darius's love, the gentle glow of the fire, and the knowledge that for the first time in a long time, both of us were safe in each other's arms.

WHEN I FELL ASLEEP IN THE ARMS OF THE MAN I LOVED, I couldn't have known we weren't out of danger just yet.

Because, how could I? *Why* would I? Darius had just said the big L-word. He wanted me to be an alpha's wife because he clearly thought I could handle the monumental responsibility. I had a thousand reservations, sure, but the Sanctius clan had welcomed me with open arms. My dragon had been crowned king. No one could touch me—theoretically. As I'd let sleep take me only hours earlier, before a crackling fire and sheltered from a furious storm, I thought, at least there, tucked against my dragon, in his *bed* that I was safe.

Not so. Another *fuck you* from the universe—one I should have seen coming when I woke abruptly from a dead, dreamless sleep one night. The room was black. The bed was comfortable.

The air was still. Yet for some reason, I was awake—and I wanted to leave.

Sighing softly, I sat up and scanned the room. Nothing. Not a thing out of place, not even with my enhanced sight. *What the hell could have woken me?* As my eyes adjusted to the darkness, my gaze caught on Darius's outline, the corded muscles across his arm, still present even at rest, and the generous dips and swells of his muscular back and shoulders. He lay on his stomach, arm over me like a snare, his face utterly at peace. His breathy snores were the only sounds punctuating the odd silence.

Carefully, I lifted his arm off me, not wanting to wake him, and clambered out of bed. After grabbing my silky black dressing gown from my luggage near the fireplace, where the embers still flickered softly, I tiptoed back, leaned across the bed, and pressed a ghost of a kiss to his temple. He stirred but didn't wake. The arm that was once around me, its weight like an ever-present security blanket, slid across the bed where I had been and nestled under the pillow. I bit back a giggle when he made some weird lip-smacking noise before resuming his snores.

As much as I wanted to rush to the door, giving in to that desire to flee like a rope tugging at my gut, trying to steer me onward, I kept my feet planted, hands on my hips, and tried to think this through. It wasn't a touch that had woken me—not a physical one, anyway. Instead, as I stood there staring around the dark room, my heart rate spiking with each worrying thought, I felt the gentle caress of *magic* wafting all around me.

It wasn't *my* magic that I felt.

In fact, it wasn't familiar in the slightest.

Back to bed, Kaye. Back to bed. My inner voice, the compass that I was beginning to suspect might be my inner, unshifted dragon, sounded distant. Hazy. Unimportant. I blinked, curious. Normally she was so clear, hovering these days at the forefront of my mind, nudging me from wrong to right. Because of that, half-asleep as I might have still been, I ignored her advice.

No one ought to be practicing magic at this hour. Catriona

would be asleep, as I knew my fae bestie required a minimum eight hours to not be a grumpy Gus the following morning. Outside of me and her, there were no other magical practitioners currently at the Sanctius clan. All those who had attended Khalon Thomas's funeral were long gone. It was just the two of us and a bunch of amazing dragon shifters.

I'd never felt more at home in all my life, even with my reservations about becoming Darius's mate.

Yet something felt... off. The longer I studied our bedroom, blanketed in darkness and calm, the straighter the hairs on the back of my neck stood. A prickling sensation skittered across my body, and I couldn't shake the feel of ants creeping up my legs, each individual little ant foot leaving its mark. Shuddering, I crossed the space, moving from a thick, woolly rug to the hard, smooth stone beneath my bare feet, grabbed for the door knob, and all but threw myself outside.

Instantly, the sensations vanished. In their place was a warm, calming magical energy that pooled in my core. I placed a hand on my stomach, blinking somewhat sleepily. While a few torches lit the way from Darius's cabin to his hall, it was far brighter out here than inside; yet another element that chased the sickly creepy-crawly feelings away.

I took a step toward the hall, the highest manmade point of the Sanctius village within the mountain landscape. With each step, however, the warmth faded. My frown deepened again, and I moved back—there was the warmth. So, this was our game. Hot and cold. I could do that if it meant answers.

So, I went off-roading, leaving the path behind and picking my way across the slate gray terrain. Normally, I'd feel the bite of the mountain underfoot: the sharp edges, the scraggly plants, the hints of old civilizations from clans gone by. Tonight, the soft undersides of my feet were immune. At one point, I paused to consider it, lifting one foot and noting the faint streaks of blood and the bits of rubble sticking into my skin. Yet the heat, so delectably comforting and pleasant in my core, spurred me on, pulsing like the crook of a finger.

So, I moved. I walked.

Bed, Kaye. No, Kaye. She tried. She really did. But my inner voice sounded as though she called to me from the foot of the mountain. Easily ignored, I drowned her out with an old lullaby hummed under my breath. Climbing, climbing, climbing ever higher—until there was nowhere left to go.

I'd reached the tip-top of the mountain, the only rocky hill higher than the alpha's hall. Above, thousands of glittering lights peered down at me, and I tipped my head back, smiling unabashedly as they put on a show. *Beautiful.* My whole body warmed further—like fire had replaced the blood in my veins, and I delighted in being burned alive.

Slowly, the stars became hazy. I blinked quickly in an effort to bring them back into focus, and soon realized there was nothing wrong with my eyes, nothing wrong with the stars, but something wrong with the air. It shimmered. *Magic.* Soft and white—gentle, yet not. Fog, yet there were hovering particles too. I gasped, watching them fly into my mouth on the wave of my breath.

Fog. Fog like the djinn.

I should have panicked right then and there, but the fire soothed me. It swathed me and lulled me back to sleep.

Run, Kaye.

I heard her this time. Like an earsplitting scream, the kind that shattered glass or started an avalanche, she begged me. Yet I couldn't run. My limbs refused to cooperate as that fog, that white dust, surrounded me, enveloped me, pervaded every entrance to my body like a parasite infecting its host.

And still the heat lingered. My mind rebelled, but my body succumbed.

The sound of boots clomping toward me forced me around, but I quickly fell to my knees, then toppled onto my side. Shoulder, head, hip—they all hit hard, though the fire blocked the pain. Slowly, with much effort, I lifted my gaze to the figure approaching, yet all I could make out was the shadow of a man. My arms, limp and outstretched, reached for him as blackness crept through my veins, extinguishing the fire. In its place—ice. I parted my lips, my mouth suddenly dry, my throat like sandpaper, but the darkness swallowed my cry.

Then, seconds later, the darkness swallowed me.

❦ 4 ❦

I FELT like I was flying—only everything hurt and the dank scent of wet, musty stone filled my nostrils with every shallow breath taken. Groaning, I tried to roll over. Tried and failed. Repeatedly. I then attempted to raise my hand to my forehead, but found my arm uncooperative.

What the hell was going on?

Had something I'd eaten at the alpha feast given me foot poisoning? Was I laying on the floor in Darius's bedroom after puking my guts out into the fireplace? Given that my body felt like it had been hit by a truck, that seemed like the most logical choice.

But why couldn't I move my arms?

Groggily, my eyes fluttered open, taking a few moments longer than I would have liked to adjust to the darkness around me. My sense of smell hadn't steered me wrong: I was, in fact, lying on a wet, cold stone floor, the ridges of each tile digging into my back. As I scanned the ceiling, the room started to spin, and I closed my eyes tightly once more, gasping in and out a few deep breaths—difficult as it was. Even with my eyes clamped shut, the room *still* seemed to spin, and my head responded in kind as a bout of nausea washed over me.

"Wha..." My lead tongue refused to move, refused to shape the syllables of the words I so desperately needed to get out. I tried to swallow, but winced at how dry everything was. Water. I needed water. Somewhere nearby, my salvation was dribbling onto the floor, but the room continued to spin when I attempted to find the source.

Kaye. Danger, Kaye. At least she could form coherent verbiage, her voice rattled around my head.

A scoff slipped out, and I finally managed to push myself onto my side, stomach roiling at what felt like a sudden movement—yet it took me at least a full minute to accomplish. Water seeped through my silk bathrobe, which lay splayed open, allowing the vengeful cold to creep across my aching body. Breathing hard, I yanked my arms up, only to discover why they had been so difficult to move: around my left wrist, an iron shackle burned into my flesh, leaving a perfectly round, red gash beneath.

Of course, it was *iron*. Let's just add insult to injury, shall we?

A panicked moan slipped out as I scrambled—and went nowhere, because there was another shackle around my right ankle. *Perfect.* Chaining me to what, I still didn't know, but what I quickly realized was that I'd been poisoned. Black lines ran along the arm that I could see, like ice water pumping through my veins. Sluggish. Weak. I'd been touched, and tricked, by a djinn.

Again.

Fortunately, I was too fucked up to panic. Too groggy to fight. My gaze swept upward, the room pulsing on either side of me, and I took in the wrought, iron cell bars a few feet away. On the other side, a figure loomed, enshrouded in darkness. My eyes narrowed, trying to make out a face, only to find a disfigured monster staring back at me. Black eyes. A drooling mouth with razor sharp teeth and gray skin. A demon? I blinked hard, hands tightening to fists, *trying* my damnedest to call upon my white magic. When I looked up again, determined not to show fear, the face had changed, morphed into a green head with red eyes and no mouth, spikes scattered across a hairless skull.

And the face continued to change, its laughter changing with it, dancing between malice and hate and genuine pleasure...

Until the poison pounding within took hold once again, dragging me back into the abyss.

WHEN CONSCIOUSNESS CAME FLOODING BACK TO ME, I STILL felt like I'd been hit by a truck, but at least I was lucid. Inhaling sharply, a blend of a gasp and a sob, I rolled onto my side and curled inward, breathing through the stiff limbs and the stabbing pain shooting up my back. Pins and needles attacked every inch of my body, stabbing and prickling as I moved each limb, down to each finger and every toe—just to prove that I could.

"You've been lying in the same position for a long time. You're bound to feel its effects, and I'm sure it isn't pleasant, but it will pass in a few minutes."

A distinctly male voice echoed all around me, and I clamped my hands over my ears, groaning. Before, from what I remembered, sickness plagued me in every sense of the word. In that moment, however, it was like experiencing a killer hangover for the first time. *Not pleasant* was the fucking understatement of the year.

Run, Kaye.

"Run where, you idiot?" I grumbled.

"What?"

"Not you." My voice caught in my supremely dry throat, each word tearing the lining apart. I paused for a moment, calling upon what depleted white magic stores I had within me to help with that. Seconds later, the pain eased, but didn't disappear— and I had nothing left to use.

Slowly, I lifted my head and found myself in a very different setting than I remembered. Sure, it was still a cell. The bars were there, but they didn't pulse with the same vomit-inducing vibrations that iron did. A quick glance at my wrist and a tug at my foot revealed I was no longer shackled, but the faded marks on my skin assured me I hadn't dreamt it. At some point, this sicko had chained me to the floor with iron.

"You were thrashing about," he noted, as if reading my mind, "so, I thought it best to keep you in one place while I treated you for the poison."

I slowly lifted my gaze to my captor, glaring so fiercely that he should have dissolved into a puddle of goo on the surprisingly dry, not wet, stone flooring. A million questions bounced around my head, incoherent and fast, but they all came to a screeching halt when I finally got a good look at him in the light of a few nearby torches. Tall. Lean. Black hair and black facial hair. Trench coat. Kind of attractive. He stood holding a white cup of steaming liquid, appraising me, his mouth twisted with annoyance—the kind of look given to a friend whose actually hungover and being a nuisance the next morning.

How dare he look at me like that.

Hector. From the funeral. The one who'd mentioned I was a hybrid during his condolence chat with Darius, speaking about me like I wasn't even there. The one who's supernatural origin I couldn't place.

"Hector," I growled, pushing my stiff body into a seated position. I also readjusted my bathrobe, unimpressed that it had been splayed open and showing off my sleep shorts and tank top. He took a quick slurp from the white Styrofoam cup, smirking.

"Aden."

"What?"

"The name's Aden," he stated, leaning his hip and shoulder against the cell bars, head cocked to one side. "For obvious reasons, I had to use a false one at the funeral."

Anger bristled through me, but I swallowed it down, knowing he'd get a kick out of seeing my emotions.

"So, I take it you didn't handle permits for Khalon Thomas either."

"No, I didn't." He swirled the contents of his cup, his eyes never leaving mine. They were almost black here, no longer arctic blue—though they were equally unnerving. "I'm a sort of... supernatural hitman, you see."

"And I'm, what, a target?" I forced a snort, as if to seem nonplussed. He took another sip, nodding.

"That's accurate, yes."

A frigid hand fisted in my stomach, clamping down and twisting. *Hello again, nausea, my old friend.*

"Why am I not dead then?" I demanded, swallowing the tremor that accompanied my words. "How many days have you had me *not* dead?"

"About six," he remarked with a quick check to the watch latched around his wrist. My eyes widened, which prompted him to shrug. "I had to wait until the poison left your system. You'd be no good to me...as you were."

"W-What poison?" A vivid image of my black veins sprung to mind—I already knew the type.

"Well..." Aden raised his hand and wiggled his fingers. One moment, his skin was pale and white, the next, it turned to a hazy blue color, fog swirling around the digits, glittering as it caught the glint of the torchlight. With a snap of his fingers, his skin returned to normal. Or maybe the blue was his normal, given he followed that with a laugh. "I'm a djinn, sweetheart. You can put two and two together."

I clutched at my stomach, willing myself not to vomit. No wonder my inner voice had been so panicked that night. She had tried to steer me back to Darius's room, but I must have been enchanted by the ridiculously powerful magic wielder standing before me.

"So, what do you want with me then? Why did you take me?" If he was about to kill me, I might as well die knowing all the facts. Not that I'd go down quietly. As soon as I sensed an attack, you bet your ass I was defending myself with whatever magic I had.

"I was hired by your dear friend, Jasmine," he purred, his face lighting up when I scowled. "Ah, yes, from that look I suspect you know her well."

I wrinkled my nose. "How could you work for her? She's probably the worst fae I've ever met."

"Yes, she is a *peach*," he said, spitting that last word in a way that told me we were on the same page as far as Jasmine was concerned. Seriously though—why couldn't she just leave me alone?

Oh.

Right.

I'd killed her uncle and foiled her grand racist plan to eliminate all shifters.

Made sense, I guessed.

"So, why haven't you done the deed?"

"Jasmine might have hired me to kill you, but she took something...rather precious from me," Aden remarked, examining his nails—bored. "Until I reacquire what she's *stolen*," I flinched at the sharpness his tone took, "I'm keeping you alive and well."

My eyebrows shot up. "Well?"

He grinned, then sighed when I continued to glare. "What? I *healed* you, didn't I? With my antidotes, there will be no lasting effects. Wipe that distain from your gaze... We have much to discuss."

"Such as?" I tried to find an exit should I somehow escape this cell, but there wasn't a window in sight and Aden was blocking the view of the hallway behind him.

"Such as, that I plan to foil her victory," he insisted, crouching down suddenly so that we were at eye level. "Such *as*, you and I are on the same side. We want the same thing."

I couldn't help it, I scoffed the most dramatic scoff I'd ever scoffed in all my life.

"You see, Jasmine has gathered much of her dear deceased

uncle's former army and plans to march on your man Darius Thomas," Aden told me. From the twisted smile on his lips, you'd think he *delighted* at the thought. I, meanwhile, had started to feel the bile creep up my throat. "Her theory was that your death would weaken the new alpha, leaving him vulnerable to her attack. It is my understanding that James Holloway and his children are also at the Sanctius village... She'll eliminate them too—"

"I have to warn them!" I cried, scrambling forward and gripping the bars of the cage. "You have to free me. If you aren't going to kill me, let me warn them about this."

"Ah, Kaye." He smirked as he stood. "That takes all the fun out of it."

"Aden—"

"Oh, save the waterworks," he snapped, spotting the tears before I felt them. "I'm not going to let her go through with it."

"Right." Like I believed that for a second. "Then why couldn't you have just pulled us aside at the funeral and *told* us? Why...this?" I gestured to the cell around me. Not a toilet in sight, I realized, yet I didn't need to relieve myself.

Creepy and gross.

"Jasmine has spies everywhere," Aden insisted, as though explaining something simple to a toddler. "I, just as much as you and your dragon, was being watched. I had to go through with it so she wouldn't suspect me. Now." He downed the rest of his drink, squished the cup, and tossed the little pieces aside. "Do you want to help me stop Jasmine or not?"

"*Obviously*."

"Good." He bounced on his toes and clapped his hands, threading those long, spindly fingers together. "I knew we'd be on the same page."

Was this guy for real? I pressed a hand to my forehead, sighing heavily and resisting the urge to remind him that I needed food, water, and other basic necessities.

"So, what's the plan then? We should alert Zayne—"

"It's too late for that," Aden muttered, brushing my suggestion off with an eyeroll. "*But*. There is an artifact rumored to have enough *power* to protect entire cities from magical harm."

I scoffed again, my hopes sinking. "Yeah, because that doesn't sound too good to be true."

"Oh, my little doubting Thomasina," the djinn said, sighing. "It was created and protected by an ancient clan of hybrids, much like yourself."

I straightened, the news causing a spike of adrenaline to hammer my tired body. "A clan of hybrids?"

"Ah, I knew that would get your attention." Aden crouched down again, wrapping his hands around the same bars I clung to, the cold wafting off his skin and onto mine. "Hybrids once ran rampant in the supernatural world, you see, but they were considered abominations. Many hunted them for sport..." He trailed off, a little sparkle in his eyes, as though remembering something especially enjoyable, followed by a quick shake of his head. "In order to protect themselves and their mates, legend goes that they created an artifact. A blend of supernatural and shifter magic. Exquisite. The first, and, sadly, last of its kind."

My hands fell into my lap. A whole *clan* of hybrids. A whole bunch of people like me—out there. Somewhere. It was hard to grasp, since everyone on Jasmine's side of things treated me like I was a first-gen mutant who needed to be squashed.

"What happened to the hybrids?" I muttered, not meeting his eye. Aden exhaled deeply, and I caught his shrug.

"No one knows. One day, they just disappeared without a trace." My heart sank the more he talked. "There are no written records, anyway, to suggest where they might have gone. Someone may have wiped them out, but I can't be sure."

"So, then how do you even *know* this stupid artifact exists?" I snapped, trying not to let my disappointment show. Aden made a face at me, as though unimpressed with my churlish attitude.

"One," he lifted a finger, "it isn't stupid. Two," he lifted another, "what does it matter? *I* have the rumored location. If it's real, as I suspect it is, don't you want to find out? Isn't it worth a shot to save your people? Your mate?"

My lips thinned, a tactic to hide the fact that any mention of Darius made my stomach loop. I had no intention of letting Aden know that, technically, Darius and I weren't mates yet, because that didn't matter to me. I loved him, whether we were bonded officially or not. Of course, I'd do whatever it took to help him.

"Or, I suppose I could let you go," Aden mused, scratching at his face scruff, "but Jasmine *has* hired others to finish the job should I fail. You can either take your chances with me... or them."

I scowled. "Gee, what a choice."

"Take it or leave it, sweet thing."

Ugh. While I *did* want to get the hell out of there, it was better to face an enemy who's face I knew rather than spend the rest of my days constantly peering over my shoulder. If this artifact could destroy Jasmine, I was going to find it.

With Aden. A djinn. Who I absolutely did *not* trust.

"So," I hesitated, knowing what came next would seal my fate, "how do we find this artifact?"

"Don't you worry your pretty little head about it," he chirped, clearly pleased with my decision. "Djinns know *all* the best treasure hordes in this realm and the next. All you need to do is follow."

"If you know where it is, why do you need me?" I demanded, brows knitted.

"It isn't just sitting out in the open," he sniped, rolling his eyes. "Hybrids built it, and hybrids protected it. There are three trials we'll need to puzzle our way through, and only a hybrid can get past them. I need you... just as surely as you need me."

So, I was supposed to take this as a win-win? Fat chance.

"Before I agree to anything, I want to speak to Darius." He must have been worried sick about me. In fact, I was pretty sure he'd rip apart Earth and Alfheim just to find me, but clearly the djinn had me locked up tightly, away from the rest of the world.

Aden studied me for a moment. While he appeared perfectly still, not even his eyes so much as flickering, I could see that brain of his churning.

"I need him to know I'm not dead," I reasoned, softening my tone in an effort to sway him. He snapped back to life with a smirk and one of those *yeah, like I'm falling for that* looks, but with a swish of his hand and a flash of blue light, a cell phone materialized in his palm. I reached out for it, but he retracted it immediately, sneering.

"What's the magic word?"

I glared. He did *not* want to know the dozens of magic words I had in mind for him.

"*Please.*" I choked out the word like it burned me, which made him snicker.

"Good girl." He passed the phone over. "Now, try not to use up all my long-distance minutes. I'm on the *worst* plan..."

"I DON'T LIKE THIS, KAYE," DARIUS GROWLED INTO THE phone. I ran a hand through my hair, nodding. Did he think *I* liked this? Not one bit. There was a djinn holding me hostage—a djinn who was probably a psychopath, but for now, I was willing to play his game.

"I know, Darius, but—"

"The artifact sounds like bullshit to me."

"Well, I mean, probably..." I caught Aden watching me from the other side of the bars, and turned slightly so my back was to him. "But what other choice do I have?"

"None, really," the djinn purred, and I rolled my eyes. It was a good thing Darius wasn't here, because the djinn would *definitely* be dead—one way or another. My dragon had been so relieved to hear from me when I finally got through to his cell, but that relief turned to white hot rage when I explained my situation. If only I could summon him through the phone, we'd get out of this thing together, just like we always did.

"Look, we can't risk not acting if what he says about Jasmine is true," I stressed, trying to keep us on track. "If she's coming for you, the clan needs to arm themselves. Tell Catriona to start making wards around the village."

"She's losing her mind over you," he muttered. I took a deep breath, not wanting to get sucked into the emotion of all this—not with Aden watching me. If the roles had switched and Catriona was the one taken hostage, I'd move mountains to find her—literally. My palms hummed with power at the thought, but I recalled the magic when Aden started clucking his tongue at me disapprovingly.

"Well, be sure to tell her I'm safe when she gets back." Apparently, James had been leading search parties all over the place, with Sanctius and Brisbane dragons scouring the skies. Catriona had finally acquiesced to Quinn's demands, using one of Hogar's newly completed saddles to ride him as she combed the country for me. Darius hadn't seen them in a few days, but messengers flitted back every so often with nothing new to report.

"Kaye, don't do this."

"I have to," I told him, my voice shaking at the desperation in his. "We don't stand a chance against Jasmine right now, not without the militia. She'll wipe you out. I won't let that happen."

"Kaye—"

"Please, Darius," I hissed. "Just *trust* me. We're still in this together, right?"

Or not at all. I waited for him to pull out, to demand that I just come home and we'd fight whatever other magical assassins Jasmine had paid to ensure my demise from the mountaintops. Instead, he exhaled deeply, and I could picture him pinching the bridge of his nose in frustration, desperation, and exhaustion.

"Together," he agreed softly. "Look, just worry about protecting your own ass, okay? Don't trust this guy."

I glanced over my shoulder. Aden waved, then tapped his wrist—apparently, I had a time limit. "You don't have to tell me twice."

"If he's lying, I'm going to rip him to pieces."

"I'd watch that movie," I said, forcing a laugh. A pointed throat clearing behind me spurred me on. "Darius, I have to go, I think. I love you. This is going to be okay."

"I love you too, Kaye," he insisted. "Trust your gut instinct. Listen to the, well, inner voices. Be safe."

"Always."

"Don't be mouthy with your captor, either. Rein in that sarcasm, for your own good."

I smiled, a genuine one this time. "I make no promises."

"Kaye..."

"I love you," I repeated, "and I..."

The phone disappeared from my hand, dissolving into nothing but blue smoke that tickled the back of my throat. I coughed, trying not to inhale it, and whirled around at the sound of the cell door sliding open.

"We're on a deadline," Aden stated, tossing a backpack at me that I only *just* managed to catch. "Things to do, places to be. Time to *go*."

"Where?" I demanded.

"Why..." His lips spread into a familiar twisted smile, the kind that made my insides turn. "Alfheim, of course..."

$$\text{❧}\quad 5 \quad\text{❧}$$

"WHAT PART of kidnapping do you not understand?" Aden snapped, his playful demeanor fading fast as we traipsed through the long, thigh-high grasses of an Alfheim field. "*No*, you cannot go see your brother. Honestly, it's like you've never been someone's captive before."

I cast a forlorn look back over my shoulder to Alfheim's Core. Despite the distance, I could make out the buildings that were being rebuilt. The smoke and ash of Abramelin's destruction was gone, and in its place, was the Alfheim I had known my whole life. In such a short time, Zayne and his people had managed to breathe life back into this place. With the sunlight beaming down on it, the city was like a paradise calling me home. Unfortunately, Aden was hellbent on dragging me in the other direction.

"But... But maybe he can *help*," I reasoned, a warm midmorning breeze tossing my loose locks this way and that. Sighing, I faced the djinn again and folded my arms over my chest. "And I've never *been* someone's captive before, thank you very much."

"No wonder you're doing such a piss-poor job at it."

"Hey." I planted my feet firmly, refusing to walk one more

step if he was going to be a raging asshole. "We're on the same team here, apparently, so how about dropping the attitude?"

"Who are you, my mom?"

When I didn't answer, he finally slowed to a halt and looked back, and threw his hands up, groaning.

"*Fine*, I'll behave," Aden called out to me, "but only if you do... and that means no detours to the Core to see Zayne Allister in his ivory tower."

"Whatever, man, *fine*." I rolled my eyes and trudged after him with my arms still crossed. "I just thought he could help."

"Help *you*, I assume."

"Help *us*," I countered, fixing him with a glare. "I thought we were a team. I thought we were working together, not that I was still your prisoner."

Aden looked toward the Core, lifting his dark gaze and grinding his teeth. He had been kind enough to let me pass through the portals without any sort of chains; I'd just assumed we were on even footing at this point. My mistake.

"Jasmine's spies are everywhere," he grunted after a terse pause. "I can't be too careful. You're my prisoner, whether you're bound or not. If I wanted, I could *make* you docile—"

"Cool." I pursed my lips, nodding. "Go fuck yourself then—"

"And they *know* that," he added under his breath, shooting me a narrowed look. "Just... Play the part, for goodness sake."

With a brusque wave, he motioned for me to follow him toward the trees. I sighed, planted my hands on my hips, and did a quick scan of the area with my enhanced sight. As far as I could tell, we were the only ones out here. Either the djinn was paranoid—or just really good at his job. I was hoping for the latter, but that didn't mean I trusted him. I did, however, appreciate that we were headed for the elvish forests rather than the ominous, foreboding death trees on the other side of the Core. But then again, it seemed more likely that elves would accept some top-secret artifact from a gang of unwanted hybrids than whatever lived in the dark forest would. Demons. Vampires.

Ghouls. That wasn't a place to go strolling through without being one of them.

Forcing the scowl off my face, I jogged after him, not bothering to waste a burst of fae speed just yet. After all, I'd only eaten a small meal since waking up—as per the doctor's orders—and I wasn't confident in the white magic I had in my reserves. For now, I needed to conserve strength, not spend it unnecessarily.

The tall grasses, a vibrant green peppered with shades of gold, brushed against my thighs, now covered in a pair of comfy, well-worn black jeans. Aden had told me to picture an outfit before we left, and suddenly I was wearing it: jeans, a cotton tee, a thin jacket, and a pair of durable walking shoes. Since I had no idea what I was in for with the search for this artifact, I wanted to be prepared for everything.

Aden waited for me at the edge of the woods, and we crossed into its shadow together. Trees similar to maples towered over us, only their trunks were fatter than any old maple found on Earth, and the undersides of their huge leaves shimmered with different colors when the breeze caught them. Every so often, we happened upon a willow tree—or whatever the Alfheim equivalent was—and I heard faint whispers of an ancient elvish dialect within. A welcome song, sweet and pure. Aden heard it too, judging from the snap of his head in the tree's direction, but he carried on gruffly, stomping across underbrush and shoving branches aside—clearly on a mission. I, however, ran my hands across the weeping branches, feeling the white magic within me swell each time. The forest had a healing touch, intentionally or not.

"So, tell me," I said after the silence had dragged on for what felt like hours. "You mentioned trials before?"

"Three trials," Aden told me over his shoulder. He stopped so abruptly that I ended up stumbling into him, and although I expected a sneer or a lewd remark, he didn't seem to notice. Instead, he looked left, then right, then left again—then made a hard right. Whatever map he was following seemed pretty specific, even if it was only the map in his mind.

"And I'm the only one who can do it?" I clarified, hurrying to his side. Someone giggled in the willow a few trees down, and I caught a flash of movement in my peripheral. Elves didn't concern me. If I felt a darker presence, I might've stopped. Elves, for all their legendary tales in human folklore, were the supernatural pacifists of our world. Mischievous, but then again, so were faes.

"They were crafted so that only a hybrid could find the artifact," Aden explained, yanking a low hanging leaf from a tree and shredding it as he walked, leaving bits behind him like breadcrumbs. "If anyone else tries, I assume nothing will happen, or something terrible will happen. I didn't want to waste my time going there either way without a hybrid."

"And these tasks—"

"Trials," he countered, throwing me a smirk as I rolled my eyes.

"Trials, whatever." I really wished that I'd imagined my hair tied back too. I seriously needed to invest in a whole tub of hair elastics one of these days. "What do they entail?"

"I'm not sure of the specifics, but there are themes," he explained, sounding slightly bored. "Strength. Wisdom. Will. You'll need to show all three traits if you want to complete the trials."

"That's all you've got? The *theme?*"

He shrugged. "Like I said, there are no written records. Much of what I'm going on comes from an oral tradition. Storytellers. Legends. But," he held a hand to silence my protest, "we djinn are stuff of legends too. I believe it. All of it."

"Great." I sighed, hoping he heard the undertones of annoyance on my breath. He had no idea what I was walking into either. So much for trying to mentally prepare for what was bound to be some bullshit. "So, beyond legend and gossip, what *do* you know?"

"I know a great many things, hybrid," he remarked, stopping again before banking hard to the left. "I've been alive a *long* time."

"Well, let's narrow it down to *this* in particular."

"I know the hybrid culture has been around for as long as there have been supernatural beings," Aden insisted. "And that hybrids, in many respects, are *better* than their supernatural or shifter components, as they often exhibit the strengths of both species. Their power is extraordinary, and I suspect *that* was why they were persecuted so mercilessly. It was fear, not a need to cleanse the bloodline, that sent their enemies after them. Hybrids, in my opinion, are the *perfect* creatures, and as such, they knew how to hide their artifact so that only one of their own could find it and use it."

For a few moments, I wasn't really sure how to respond to that. In my limited experience of being a hybrid, no one had ever said I was the perfect creature. I was a mongrel, a dog, an abomination to my enemies. And to my community, my mixed heritage was ignored—like I'd spent my entire life walking around with a huge piece of spinach in my teeth that no one cared to point out. Aden was the first person, beyond Catriona's comforting words and Darius's unflinching love, to praise what I was, and in that moment, I started to soften toward him.

But I put a halt to that *really* fast. No way was I letting this guy trick me into lowering my guard. I was still his prisoner, after all, and just because he felt something other than hatred for hybrids didn't change that.

"If hybrids are so perfect, why are there none of us around anymore? Why am I such a taboo subject?"

He shot me a look over his shoulder, brow furrowed. "Weren't you listening? They were stamped out. Persecuted out of fear. Do you really think they would stick around? The supernatural community is massive these days. With crazies like Abramelin and Jasmine surfacing, in what universe do you think a hybrid community, if they did still exist, would show themselves? Use your brain, Kaye."

"Okay, rude," I snapped. "I'm still new to this. You don't have to be a dick."

"Pretty sure that's my family motto," he said with a chuckle. "Being a dick is in my blood."

"Fine, change of subject then." I wanted to regain the upper hand here, and clearly hybrid lore was this djinn's special interest project, though I couldn't understand why. To me, he was full djinn. Was it the power thing? Maybe he wanted a slice of it. With Aden smirking back at me, I cleared my throat and lifted an eyebrow. "What did Jasmine take from you?"

In a heartbeat that victorious smirk fell, and in its place... contempt. Aden turned away and quickened his stride.

"It doesn't matter what she took from me," he growled, and I noticed his fingertips pulsing a faint blue color.

"Well, it kind of sets the tone for this whole thing," I insisted, running to keep up with him. "Right? I mean, is this a vengeance mission, or are you genuinely interested in saving shifter clans from the awful that is Jasmine?"

"It's none of your business."

"But we're a team, so technically, it *is*—"

"I have no interest in sharing my personal details with you," he snapped. His right hand, curled in a tight fist, had turned completely blue at this point. I wasn't an idiot, nor did I have a death wish, so I backed off, hands up in surrender.

"Fine. You don't have to tell me if it upsets you that much."

We continued walking for a few paces before he started to slow down. Finally, he glanced over at me, his hands no longer glowing with djinn essence, and nodded. "Thank you."

I frowned. It had been a long time since I had struggled this hard to get a read on a person. Even Darius, despite all the ways he drove me nuts when we first met, was easier to read than this. Alpha male with wounded pride. Protective to a fault. Born leader. He had all the classic traits—and I loved him for it.

Aden? Maybe he fell into the mythological trickster category, but there was rage simmering just below the surface.

And at that point, as we trekked through elvish territory in a tense silence, I couldn't decide whether I wanted to poke the sleeping bear or not, just to see what might become of it.

Oh, who was I kidding?

Give me a stick already. Of course, I was going to poke.

CROUCHED AT THE EDGE OF THE GLITTERING POOL, ADEN trailed his fingers through the water, then looked back at me with a grin. "I'm going to say... no iron."

"Bullshit."

"*Why* would I feel the need to bullshit you?" he asked, wiping his hand on his trousers before standing. His trench coat hem grazed the water's edge, and he hastily yanked it out of reach.

I crossed my arms, staying back at a good distance and eyeing the pool suspiciously. "Because you think it'd be funny to watch a fae interact with iron? I don't know. Pretty sure you've done it before." I held up my wrists, a very faint red ribbon of burned flesh still wrapped around each, to emphasize my point.

"Half-fae," he corrected, his grin turning a little wicked as I exhaled sharply. "And why would I want to weaken you? Night's coming. Darkness is fraught with all sorts of beasties, even in elven lands."

My gaze darted skyward. Sure enough, the sun was on its way down, and we had spent the better part of the day hiking. I'd asked repeatedly why we couldn't just fly there—djinns were known to materialize out of nowhere, so I had to assume there was some magical transportation up his sleeve that would be faster. Aden had merely countered that he didn't want to miss the entrance of the tomb, which made me feel fan-fucking-tastic. Not only were we hunting an artifact that we weren't totally sure existed, and not only were there three trials that *only*

I could supposedly solve, but we were going to desecrate a super-natural tomb too.

Not exactly my idea of a good time.

"Oh, for goodness sake," he groaned, stalking toward me. "The water is *safe*."

"I don't—" Before I could express my rightful doubts, he flicked his fingers at me, spraying whatever water was left at my face.

"See?" He cocked his head to the side, grinning. "Perfectly safe."

Rather than flip him off like I wanted to, I curled my hands into fists and stalked to the edge of the water. While my face wasn't dotted with burns, that didn't mean I could trust him. Still, the sun had been hot all day, the water looked refreshing, and I wouldn't have minded dunking my head under the surface for a bit, if only to get some clarity. So, I peeled off my jacket and walking shoes. Setting them in a neat pile beside me, I stuffed my socks into my shoes, rolled up my jeans as best I could, and stuck my feet in.

Beautiful. Cool. Revitalizing. Not a trace of iron present. Just what my exhausted feet needed after today. I wasn't sure how long we planned to stay here, or what Aden had in mind for food, but I didn't want to spoil the moment by asking. Instead, I dragged my feet through the water, its surface a nearly perfect mirror. Taking a moment, I studied my reflection, noting that even though I'd been poisoned, I didn't look terrible. All things considered, I'd take that as a win.

Suddenly, a figure joined my reflection in the pool—and it wasn't Aden. My eyes widened, but before I could react, a lead-soled foot booted me into the water, kicking me in the middle of my back. The muddy bank gave way and the water embraced me like I was a long-lost child, falling into its depths before I had a chance to gulp down a breath. I kicked for the surface, only to be met with two huge hands on my shoulders, holding me under.

Fuck this. I'd survived a fatal djinn poisoning—twice; I was not about to die today because some asshole wanted to drown me. Clamping down on my attacker's wrists, I emitted a surge of white magic. At such close range, it would feel similar to a flame licking the skin, and although slightly muffled, I heard a scream above the surface. His grip loosened, and I managed to push off the muddy bottom and shoot for the surface. When I breached it, sucking in air as hard as I could, I found Aden dragging my assailant away from the pool, an arm locked around his neck.

A demon. I front-crawled for the water's edge and lifted myself out.

"Another assassin," Aden grunted, struggling to keep the monster down. He tightened his chokehold, teeth gritted. "I told you they were everywhere."

Red eyes glowered back at me, ashen skin stretched thin over protruding bones, lifting to reveal razor sharp teeth. The demon thrashed about, then snatched a serrated blade from his belt and thrust it back and up, but Aden managed to dodge it. His lithe body moved with surprising grace—like a dancer.

"Fucking Jasmine," I hissed, ready to blast this creep into the next realm. "Lemme at him."

Just as I raised my hands, magic gathering in my palms, an arrow whizzed toward me from the trees. I dodged just in time, feeling the faint brush of its black feathers against my cheek. The next one launched my way was met with a wall of magic, which it bounced off and disintegrated on the spot. Stalking across the soft grasses, I left Aden to grapple with the demon, knowing a djinn was more than an even match. Then I hurled a disorientating hex at the dark elf perched on the branches of a massive maple lookalike. *Okay*, so apparently, not every elf was a supernatural pacifist. The creature toppled from the tree and landed in a heap at the bottom. His navy-purple hair obscured his features, though I knew in an instant from the silvery skin that this was a dark elf from the haunted forest.

Apparently, they were a team. Either that or *two* of Jasmine's hired assassins had found us at the same time. Maybe Aden wasn't full of shit when he lectured me about spies being everywhere.

Before he could get his bearings, I hit the elf with another hex, and this time the force of it slammed his head into the tree trunk, rendering him unconscious. Good. Fucker.

"Kaye!"

At the mild panic in Aden's voice, I whirled around, the world stuttering into slow motion. There, some ten feet away, was the demon—upright and free. He hurled that jagged blade at me, his aim straight and true. Over and over and knife flipped, as though clawing its way through the air to claim its victim. My arms shot up to block, but I knew it wasn't fast enough.

Drop, Kaye. Drop!

Then, blue fog materialized in front of me, slowly, filling the space, blocking me. The blade cycled closer. The fog became a man. The blade found its target.

The world came crashing back to full speed in the blink of an eye, and Aden dropped to his knees before me, the blade embedded in his chest.

"Aden!"

The demon sneered, but one step toward me earned him an eviscerating curse straight to the gut. He stumbled back as black blood spilled down his body before crashing into the pool.

"Oh, my god," I stammered, dropping down and carefully rolling Aden onto his back. "What were you *thinking*?!"

"The hybrid can't die," he managed through gritted teeth, maroon blood spilling over his lips as he spoke. "*You* are the key to... to finding it..."

"And *you* have the map, you idiot," I snapped. I had no right to be angry with him, of course, but it was the first emotion that surfaced. Fear and panic were a close second and third, followed swiftly by gratitude. He had thrown himself in harm's way to save me. Maybe I could have avoided the knife, but while it wouldn't have buried itself in my chest, it might have hit my shoulder.

Unwilling to lose him after such a sacrifice, I told him to shut up—he kept rambling on about how I had to save her, save *them*, and I couldn't concentrate on healing him with all that pressure on my shoulders. Slowly, carefully, I removed the blade, blocking out his cries, and pressed a hand over the gushing wound. Tossing the blade aside, its aura riddled with dark magic, I set to work on saving him. White, healing magic poured out of me, one hand over his wound, the other on his forehead. In my mind's eye, I saw the white light suturing the wounds, closing the shredded muscle, and stopping the gushing blood, until finally Aden gasped. He drew in an enormous breath, his chest rising swiftly beneath my hand, and rolled over, hacking up a storm.

"Thank you," he croaked, as I collapsed onto my backside, wiping the dark purple blood on my pants. My heart raced and my mind became a blur. Exhaustion threatened to set in, so I flopped back to catch my breath.

"Now we're even," I told him. He shuffled across the grass so that we lay next to each other.

"Now I *trust* you," he countered. "Seriously. Thank you. I could've died if you wanted me to."

I bit the insides of my cheeks for a moment. "Well, we're on the same team, right? Nobody on my team gets left behind."

And maybe, just maybe, the djinn had shown why he might just be trustworthy after all.

I closed my eyes and willed my body to calm down.

No. The jury was still out on the whole trust thing.

For now.

✾　6　✾

"So, you're cool with just breaking into and desecrating a tomb?" I asked, my eyes widening as they adjusted to the darkness. I mean, *yes*, Darius and I had gone rooting through a graveyard back when we were first searching for Zayne, but that was different. The grave we eventually settled on wasn't a grave at all, but a secret passageway down to the Hive.

"It's not a real tomb, Kaye," Aden insisted. Although I couldn't see them, I could easily hear his hands smoothing along the walls of the long, dark tunnel we suddenly found ourselves in. Dirt, wet leaves, and something vaguely manure-y filled my nostrils, and I opted for breathing through my mouth. A good fifty feet behind us, the partially opened wooden doorway let some of the dying light filter in, but soon it would be just as dark in the forest as it was in here.

Mercifully, we'd only needed to hike half the day to find the tomb, excluding our rendezvous with Jasmine's assassins in the woods. The demon had bled out and sunk to the bottom of the pool. We had handed the dark elf over to a band of curious light elves, who accepted our gift with devious grins, dragging his unconscious body into an opening at the base of a weeping willow.

"Sure feels like a real tomb," I muttered. "What stinks?"

"I don't know," Aden said, sighing. "Death?"

"You said—"

"Just because it isn't a *real* tomb doesn't mean people haven't died in here."

I rolled my eyes at the sound of his trademark scoff. This djinn, despite taking a metaphorical bullet for me not all that long ago, was forever unimpressed with my ignorance.

"Perfect."

"You think we're the only ones who've come looking for this rumored artifact? Ah, here we go..." Moments later, bursts of light popped up along the walls—the torches seeming to ignite on their own. I knew better. A pulse of magic so powerful it made my knees weak washed over me, crashing in both directions like a tidal wave, igniting torches as it went. Djinns. Never to be underestimated, even if I had saved one from dying. The guy standing before me was a powder keg of magic. I, on the other hand, had only just recouped all the white magic I spent healing him, but given that he'd nearly died to save me in the first place, I couldn't hold it against him.

Aden dusted his hands on his trench coat, then looked back at me. "Shall we?"

I nodded. Although my inner voice hadn't uttered a whispered warning in a while, I couldn't help but wonder if this was all some elaborate trap to murder me in a tomb. Maybe this was supposed to be *my* tomb?

I shook my head. *No.* If I allowed myself to wander down that road, I might as well make a run for it now and try my luck with the unknown.

This was for Darius. This was for the Sanctius clan. If the artifact really could protect them, *and* we found a way to potentially replicate it, shifter communities around the world could be kept safe from marauding assholes like Jasmine and her goons.

We hadn't walked all that far before arriving at our first obstacle: a giant boulder blocking the passageway in its entirety.

Almost, anyway. Around the edges, light flickered, suggesting an opening behind it. I stood back with my hands on my hips, as Aden pressed an ear to the boulder, running his hands over it, eyes closed.

"Can you hear the ocean?" I asked, smirking when he glared.

"This is it. The first challenge."

"Trial?"

"Whatever." He took a few steps back, nodding. "Look, *there.* You see? The glyph?"

I moved in closer, squinting. There, in the dead middle of the boulder, was a single carved glyph. Much to my surprise, it was an old fae symbol for power, or, in some interpretations, strength.

"I think we need to move it," I remarked, stepping back to appraise the enormous obstacle with a sigh. Out of the corner of my eye, I caught Aden shaking his head in disbelief.

"No kidding." He offered two sarcastic claps. "*So* glad I brought you along. Sheer genius—"

"Oh my god, shut up." Carefully, I placed just the tips of my fingers against the boulder. When no electrical current raced up my arms, I pushed harder. "Help me move this thing then."

"On to that," Aden noted with a nod.

On the floor, off to the side, totally inconspicuous, sat a raised panel. Aden pushed at it with his foot, and while I heard a rush of click-click-*click*ing in the walls, nothing happened. The djinn huffed, then came to my side and squatted low. "I suspect our weights won't be enough to trigger a release. The rock needs to go on the panel. Probably to open a door of some kind."

Still annoyed at his unhelpful sarcasm earlier, I gritted my teeth and tried to lift, push, and pull when he did. We tried every angle we could, coming at it from all sides, but none of our efforts paid off. The damn thing wouldn't budge, not even with a surge of magic from both of us.

"Inconceivable," Aden grumbled, a bead of sweat rolling

down from his hairline when we stepped back. "I have super-human strength. This... is perhaps not meant to be moved."

I winced when that sweat droplet rolled right into his eye, but the djinn seemed not to notice. Instead, he turned his full attention to me, a glimmer of madness twinkling in those black orbs.

"Shift," he ordered. "Our combined strengths, you as a dragon, should be enough to move it."

I blinked rapidly, suddenly flustered. "I..."

"If the nudity bothers you, I won't look." He placed a hand over his eyes, but peeked through his fingers, smirking. "Pinky promise. Come on, now. Give us a show."

"I can't shift," I admitted softly, and his arm dropped to his side. "I don't... I can't do it yet."

Especially not on command. Besides, the first time I shifted would *not* be with Aden. I wanted my first shift to be with Darius, if it ever happened at all.

"Are you serious?" Never had he looked so unimpressed with me—and that was saying something. "You can't shift?"

"It's complicated." My eyes narrowed when his features morphed into something more along the lines of annoyed. "Try something else."

Before he could argue, I turned away and scanned the torchlit corridor. Roots and cobwebs lined the ceiling, and damp dirt made up the floor. Another push at the panel yielded nothing, and behind me, Aden appeared to be using everything in his magical arsenal against our boulder foe. No dice. Nibbling my lower lip, my scrutiny moved onto the torches themselves, their flames dancing in a wind I couldn't feel.

Concerning.

Beyond that, however, I noted that the structure of the torches themselves were made of metal—long, thick metal poles, in fact.

The sort that could be used for leverage when lifting an insanely heavy object.

"Aden…" I rushed forward and yanked a torch off the wall, pulling a massive chunk of earth and dust with it. Extinguishing the flame on the floor, I held the metal bar up, grinning. "Lever?"

The djinn stared at me for a moment, eyebrows twitching downward, and then rushed for another torch. We then stuffed the ends under the boulder as best we could and situated ourselves so that if we managed to lift it, the relatively round rock should roll straight onto the panel.

"One," Aden said, meeting my gaze. I nodded.

"Two."

"*Three*," we said in unison. Seconds later, our grunts and groans filled the corridor as we pushed down on our makeshift levers with all our might. Still, the boulder refused the move. A string of Arabic curses flew out from the djinn's mouth, and I had to bite my cheeks to keep from laughing. Sure, I was frustrated too, but I preferred watching *him* lose his cool. Besides, Arabic swearing was hilarious. *You mother goat fucker*? Hilarity. Perhaps, he'd forgotten that faes were blessed with the gift of gab—language comprehension came easy for all of us, even if we'd never heard the dialect before.

Sweaty, hot, and more than a little upset, we took a break a few minutes later. Aden let go of his lever first, and suddenly the boulder moved. Barely, but with my hand still slightly pushing down on my metal pole, it twitched.

"Wait," I said, realization hitting me like a baseball bat to the head. *I* was the one who needed to pass these trials. "*Wait*. You said the hybrid is the only one who can do these trials. I… Don't touch it!"

Aden stepped back from his pole, hands raised, and I seized the moment to prove my worth. Pushing down on the lever with all my might, I let out a victorious cry when the boulder moved, rolling out of the way like it weighed next to nothing. I managed to guide it onto the panel, and a series of loud clicking, clanking, and knocking erupted around us. Moments later, a door embedded in the wall creaked open some ten feet behind us.

"You were right before," I sneered, yanking another lit torch off the wall and heading for the door. "You *should* be glad you brought me. Sheer genius."

"Indeed," Aden muttered. His lips twitched into a little half smile, and he followed me through the dark doorway, my torch lighting the way.

One trial down, two to go.

$$\text{❀} \quad 7 \quad \text{❀}$$

THE HALL STEERING us from the first trial to the second was a tight fit. In fact, slowly, the walls seemed to be closing in on us, and the air thickened with the scent of wet dirt and dead flesh. Gripping my torch tightly, I took one last deep breath, then shot off with a very gentle burst of fae speed. Behind me, Aden shouted my name, and I knew I should have been more cautious, but I *had* to get out of there—immediately.

I stuttered to a crashing halt, however, when I came flying out of the claustrophobic hallway and into a dark room, lit only by a chandelier made up of candles hanging from the ceiling. Wax dripped slowly down the stalks, then fell to the floor like rain, hardening on impact. A chill ran up my spine, and I gasped at the sight of a specter hovering directly across the room from me.

"For fuck's sake, Kaye," Aden growled, his footfalls barely making a sound as he caught up to me. "We need to stick together in here!" His hand clamped down on my shoulder, but I didn't even flinch. "You never know what kind of boobytraps those hybrids set. You could have been *impaled* moving at that speed, and then where would I be? Shit out of luck, just like your dragon—"

"Shut. Up. Aden," I hissed through gritted teeth. He stepped around me, his glaring eyes not leaving my face—until he must have felt it too. The chill. The *presence*. His features went slack, and slowly, he turned around to face the shimmering ghost on the other side of the room. I swallowed hard and gripped the torch firmly—not like it would do much against a ghost. Suddenly, the flame extinguished, and my breath fogged before me.

"Is that—"

"A ghost?" I offered. "Maybe. Is this the next trial?"

The djinn seemed just as unsure as I felt, and I watched him take in the otherwise empty room, his gaze lingering on the chandelier for a moment.

"Possibly. The next trial is... wisdom."

With no glyphs in sight, not like the one I saw etched into the boulder, I stepped forward cautiously. However, as soon as I'd taken a single step, the specter's eyes snapped up, honing in on me.

In life, she must have been beautiful, this ghost. In death, hauntingly so. Dark straight hair flowed down her back, forever touched by an unseen wind, fluttering delicately. Her dress, fitted around the waist before exploding out into some ballgown monstrosity, appeared moth-eaten and torn. It too shifted about, as though caught in a breeze. Once again, I felt no wind, no soft caress of nature against my skin.

Cold gripped me, latching onto the tips of my fingers and numbing them. Drawing a deep breath, I flexed my hands and took a few more steps toward her. She didn't move, yet her sad eyes followed me curiously, her full lips slightly parted. Her feet, I noted in the brief moment that the unseen breeze lifted her dress, were bare.

"Hello," I said carefully.

Aden crept along beside me, his magical aura notched up to high; clearly, he thought we were about to set off a trap. While the hum of his power tickled my ears, I managed to block it out and focus strictly on the ghost. If this was the next trial, she was the key. Slowly, the woman dipped her head in greeting, hovering a foot or so above the ground.

Danger? I asked my inner voice, my steps slow and precise. I avoided the chandelier, opting to move around it rather than under it, though somehow wax still managed to land on my shoulder.

No, came her unusually soft reply. *No danger, Kaye. Only him.*

I tried not to smile. I guess I wasn't the only one who still didn't completely trust the djinn skulking along beside me.

Well. She was me and I was her, yet I couldn't help but think of her as a separate being.

"Greetings, Kaye Allister," the specter murmured. I stilled, noting that her lips didn't move as she spoke, yet her voice seemed to fill the room. Melodic and soft, girlish yet not, it bore the weight of one who had witnessed tragedy and experienced agony. A quick glance to Aden told me that he heard the voice too, that it wasn't just in my head. The ghost stared at me, yet straight *through* me too, her voice swelling once more. Clear, crisp—like a stage actress on the night of her big debut. "Daughter of fae and dragon. You have survived the first trial."

I gulped. Was there an option *not* to survive? I had been under the impression failures simply couldn't move the boulder. Maybe there was something darker waiting in the shadows if we had continued to strike out.

"Is this the second trial?" Aden asked, his tone surprisingly civilized. The ghost continued to hover and flutter, and not once did her gaze shift to the djinn. He groaned, then nudged me. "Apparently, I'm not even here."

"Wouldn't that be something," I muttered before stepping toward her. I gave us a good five-feet of separation, as that was about all the cold I could handle. Clearing my throat, I repeated Aden's question, and when the ghost nodded, I let out a soft sigh. "Okay. Good. Wisdom. Let's do this."

She seemed momentarily perplexed by my response.

"Can you help me?" My fingers wanted to fidget, to move, to expel all the nervous energy pumping through my limbs, but I forced them to remain still. Something told me I'd need to at least pretend to be confident during these trials, even if that was the farthest thing from reality.

"My story begins in an age gone by," the ghost said, sighing through her words. Briefly, she almost sounded wistful. "I was your age when I died, but before I did, I was offered a choice. My mate or my child."

I fought back a shiver, quickly piecing together what I might need to do—and praying that wasn't the case. An image of Darius in trouble, his life hanging by a thread, flickered across my mind like old movie footage—but, then I reminded myself I had no child, so maybe I was wrong.

"Both were bound in chains," she told me, her wistfulness turning hard and the temperature around us dropping even further. Behind me, I heard the faint chatter of Aden's teeth as the poor creature relayed her tale. "I was forced to choose. Save the life of only one... and kill the other."

Tears sprang to my eyes suddenly, though I managed to blink them away. What a *choice*. One that I would be forced to make given the way the specter's haunting eyes stared deeply into mine.

"What would you do, Kaye Allister?" She drifted listlessly toward me, the torn bits of dress fabric floating along behind her. "Who would you choose to save?"

Each inhale seared down my throat, the air bitterly cold. I held firm, even as she closed in on me, her head tipped to one side.

No one should have to choose between their soulmate and their child. But the morality of the situation didn't matter. It wasn't a topic of discussion. *This* was the trial. I bowed my head for a moment, considering the two options—even though I knew my answer the second she posed the question. I wanted to take the time given to weigh my response, to draw upon whatever wisdom I had inside of me to make the right decision.

For all my thinking, I couldn't find a reason to change my gut instinct.

"I'd save our child," I told her, pleased that my voice held firm. As much as I loved my dragon, I couldn't butcher our child, nor would I *ever* let anyone else lay a hand on him or her. Darius would understand, and, I suspected, would make the same decision should he be faced with the same impossible choice.

The specter nodded solemnly. "As did I. Yet when our captor handed me the dagger, and I plunged it into the heart of my mate... my child's heart bled, red spilling from her chest. Dripping onto the floor. Drip, drip, *drip*."

Like the candle wax. I forced back my tears; this woman had truly suffered before her end.

"What did I do wrong?" the ghost whispered, her voice sweeping over me causing my skin to erupt in little goosebumps. "Where was my error?"

"You didn't make an error," I insisted, but I knew that wouldn't do her any good. She blinked back at me, stoic and silent, and I took a few moments to think her predicament through. In the end, I shook my head and relayed the only conclusion that made sense. "You were betrayed. Whoever was holding you captive tricked you. You... You shouldn't have trusted them."

How similar to my own situation. Would there be a moment in the near future when the small bit of trust I'd put in Aden proved to be my downfall?

The ghost smiled, as if pleased with my answer, but I wouldn't call it a happy smile. Tinged with sorrow, it didn't reach her eyes.

"What would you have done differently, Kaye Allister?"

I bit my lip to keep the first thing that came to my mind from tumbling out. Logically, I'd say that I would stab my child. In the described situation, that would mean my mate died and the child lived. Yet, I couldn't bring myself to say it—because in reality, I wouldn't do either of the two options. The more I thought about it, the more I realized that if I were faced with that choice, I'd turn the knife on myself and save the two beings in this world that I loved more than anything. We all think we're brave enough, bold enough, level-headed enough, to do the logical thing. But in the heat of the moment, I knew where I would really stick that knife.

"I wouldn't choose either," I admitted softly. "I'd take my own life to save theirs. I... I'd use the knife on myself."

After a tense moment of silence passed, the specter retreated, dragging the cold with her. I wiggled my toes, but I still couldn't feel them.

"Sacrificing your own life to save the ones you love is noble," the ghost told me, her tone suddenly brighter, warmer. "It is *wise*. Sacrificing another to save yourself, to save but a single life, is cowardice."

Then, with a gentle *pop*, she disappeared. The cold vanished. The scent of death lifted. I whirled around as the room brightened, the chandelier morphing from candle to modern crystal. Even the droplet of wax on my shoulder was gone.

"What—"

"You've passed the trial," Aden stated, his voice thick. "Look."

Where the ghost last stood, a door swung open allowing a knee-high cloud of mist to slowly filter into the room.

"Two down," I said with a nod. "Okay. This isn't so bad."

A glance back at Aden's face suggested otherwise. Expression unreadable, he stalked toward the door without a word, and I followed, my brow furrowed in confusion.

"Are you okay?"

"I'm fine," he snapped. "The story... It got to me, that's all."

"What would you have chosen?" I couldn't help myself. Now that the ghost was gone, it wouldn't matter what he said. Aden stopped sharply just before passing through the doorway, and the look in his black eyes sent a shiver down my spine.

"I wouldn't choose," he growled. Blue light raced around his fingers, his skin peeling back to reveal the true djinn hiding beneath. "I'd kill anyone who threatened my family. It would be a bloodbath."

I gulped. "Noted."

Another layer revealed, and while my suspicions as to what Jasmine had stolen were starting to narrow down, I realized I still knew nothing about the creature leading me into the abyss.

And that frightened me more than I cared to admit.

8

CautiousLY, Aden and I picked a path through the swirling mist. The white, ever-rolling fog was so difficult to see through that neither of us knew exactly what we walked on, so caution was key. However, every step felt like stone underfoot. At one point, Aden tripped and stumbled forward, and I darted forward to keep him from faceplanting into the fog.

"Stairs," he grumbled, and we climbed them one at a time, slowly, until we reached the top. There, the corridor opened up into yet another room. I placed a hand on the wall before entering, closing my eyes briefly and feeling the thrum of magic within. At this point, I had no idea where we were relative to the elvish forest outside, but I had to think our current reality was warped and skewed by whatever magical entrapments the hybrids had lain. The magic didn't feel dark to me—its vibrations humming across my skin—but it didn't strike me as white magic either. Perhaps something in the murky middle. I withdrew quickly at the thought, clenching and unclenching my hand to get rid of the phantom tremors that remained.

"Kaye? I'm not really sure what to make of this..."

I followed the sound of his voice into the room, then stopped and looked around, my mouth hanging open. This chamber was the largest yet. Created entirely of red clay, it stood tall and rectangular, the ceiling so far up that I couldn't even see it; the only reason I even knew there was a ceiling was the fact that sunlight hadn't touched my skin since we entered the tomb —and yet, the room wasn't dark. Something unseen illuminated the vast space. In the center of it all, a small hill spiraled upward some thirty feet into the air. It was steep, no stairs, and there appeared to be a table on top. I spied Aden's boot prints in the clay path.

"Here goes nothing," I muttered, following his steps to the very top. As I'd thought, there was a table, yet the silk fabric draped over it suggested that it might be an altar of some kind. A candle burned on either side, and at its center sat a golden chalice and a thin, silver dagger.

"This *should* be the trial of your will," Aden said, running a fingertip around the edge of the chalice, "but I don't... see the connection."

"Your guess is as good as mine." I grabbed the goblet, carefully wrapping my hand around it. When nothing electrocuted me and no enormous spikes came careening down from the ceiling, I brought it to my nose and sniffed. Blood-red liquid sloshed around inside, equal to half a glass of wine. "It doesn't smell like anything."

"Looks delicious."

My lips twitched into a little smile, pleased that his scary I'll-kill-the-world side had been left behind at the second trial. "Bet it goes great with steak."

"Or, you know, it'll sear a hole in your throat as soon as you drink it."

Great. I shot him a narrowed look. "Seriously?"

"Okay, okay, sorry," he said, clearing his throat and fighting a smirk. "I'll be more supportive. I'm sure it's fine. You've already passed the wisdom trial... It's unlikely they'd trick you here. You've proven, in theory, that you're not a total moron."

What I wouldn't give to punch him squarely in the nose—

just once. His lopsided grin almost fooled me into thinking he was on my side, but I knew, deep down, he probably thought I actually *was* a total moron.

Well. A total moron wouldn't have figured out the last two trials while an all-powerful djinn floundered around beside her.

Squaring my shoulders, I lifted the chalice in his direction. "Well. Cheers."

"I'll do what I can if things go awry," Aden told me as I brought the golden rim to my lips. I paused, resisting the urge to splash the blood-like liquid inside all over his face—you know, just to see if things went awry. Aden pushed the chalice toward me, fingertips tipping the bottom up as I scowled.

Kaye...

Too late for your protests now, inner voice. Ignoring all sense of reason and self-preservation, I drained the chalice dry. Sure enough, just as the liquid didn't smell like anything, it lacked taste too. Lukewarm, it trickled down my throat and left an oily residue behind, the kind I felt every time I swallowed.

"Well?" Aden raised his eyebrows as he looked me over. "No hole burning into your throat?"

"No." I smacked my lips together. "But it leaves a bit of a weird slime in my mouth, so..."

I trailed off as something twitched within me. A prickle of *ouch*, almost like that of an insane period cramp. It flexed in my lower abdomen, and my hand hovered over the affected area as it continued to pulse with pain.

"Kaye?"

"Just... Gimme a second," I muttered. Another beat of pain. This time, it felt like someone had sunk a hook into all my internal organs in that area, found a spot to stand somewhere in the middle, and *yanked* hard on all the strings. A cry crept up my throat, croaking out of me at the next tug. The chalice fell from my hand and started rolling down the red clay path I'd climbed to reach the altar. The next pulse sent the pain snaking up my stomach, then surging up my throat—like heartburn times a million. I crumpled to the ground, shrieking.

"Kaye!" Aden knelt down and tried to straighten me out, but I pushed him away as the agony radiated out through my arms. An invisible fist clamped down around my heart, and I doubled over, coughing. Blood splattered across my hands. The pain had reached my toes now, steadily encompassing my entire body until I was nothing but pain. It alternated between stabbing and slicing, and through my tears I weakly looked myself over, expecting there to be gaping wounds and holes, with blood spilling from me at every turn.

But there was nothing.

It was all inside. A blend of a gasp and a sob slipped out of me. Fire coursed through my veins, burning me alive. I'd felt fire before. I'd reveled in it. But this was different. This fire was a beast of its own mind, and it wanted to devour me from the inside out.

"M-Make it s-stop," I pleaded, grasping at Aden's trench coat, another wail ripping from my throat as the pain intensified.

"This is a test. It is *will*, Kaye. You have to fight it! You have to endure it!"

"I c-can't!" My voice hitched in my throat, a throat that felt like a thousand knives slid down it every time I managed to swallow.

"You can," Aden said firmly, lifting my head by my chin, his dark eyes boring into mine. "I *know* you can. You're stronger than this, Kaye. Remember, *you* are the perfect creature. Superior to all of us. You can survive this!"

"Stop talking!" I cried, clamping my hands down over my ears. Each word he spoke rattled around my head like he'd screamed it through a bullhorn. Every touch, taste, sound— magnified, as though only to enhance the pain.

You can end this, a voice murmured, the slithery hiss of its words reverberated inside my skull. For a fleeting moment, clarity reigned supreme, and I pushed my hair out of my face, sniffling.

"W-What?"

"I didn't say anything," Aden grumbled, still crouched on his haunches before me. "Kaye, what's happening?"

You can end the pain. I waved him off with a frown, needing to listen to this voice, this stranger inside my head. It wasn't my inner voice. The pain drowned her out. But this... A man's voice, akin to a dull roar over the tsunami of agony pounding me over and over again.

The knife...

A sob slipped out as my gaze wandered back to the altar. I pointed weakly, even the slight motion of uncurling my finger was enough to march a fiery hailstorm through my body. Aden's brow furrowed, as if not understanding, and when I choked out the word, he shook his head.

"Kaye, no—"

"Get me the knife!" I doubled over again, my hands hovering over my ears as my words echoed through the red, clay hall. I'd never experienced this kind of burning agony before, like my skin was ready to bubble up and explode. Pressure compounded inside my head, pushing against the confines of my skull, a sharp, stabbing hurt festering behind my eyes.

Out of nowhere, the silver blade slid into my hand, and I looked up slowly. Aden peered back at me, his worry apparent.

Take the knife. I gripped it, wishing the cool metal might offer some release. The movement only made my knuckle crack and pop out of place. *Stab it into your heart. End the pain. End the suffering.*

In that moment, I couldn't deny it was tempting. Slowly, I raised the blade's tip to the center of my chest, pressing it over my heart. My cotton tee managed to cushion the blade's bite, but not for long. I felt it. Over all the pain, the twisted suffering, I felt the blade. Wherever it touched, the ache eased. It was my salvation.

All I had to do was die.

"Kaye, what are you...?"

Plunge the blade into your heart. End the suffering.

"N-No," I argued, but my protests sounded weak even to my own ears. The pain was devastating—but I wasn't ready to die in order to end it.

Or was I? As the sharpness spiked across my body, my bones felt like they were breaking, yet when I looked down, they remained intact. All I got was the pain of it, the breathtaking torture without the act itself.

Do it. Save yourself.

"No," I choked, this time my answer was clear. *Hadn't I proven I wouldn't save myself already?* I forced my thoughts to drift to Darius, to his smile, to his stormy gray eyes. I remembered how he kissed me, the summer rain raging wildly around us. I thought of his tender care, his warm hand on my forehead as I shivered through cold sweats, expelling the djinn's poison from my system.

I didn't want to die. I wanted to live—to endure, to fight on for the ones I loved most in this world.

I wanted to live to become his wife, his partner.

His mate.

His queen.

Do it! The dull roar had upgraded to booming thunder, the hissing voice rattling my brain as the pain reached a crescendo.

"No!" I screamed back, then hurled the knife with all my might, tossing it off the edge of the altar's peak. Teeth gritted, I buckled down to ride out the pain, thinking of Darius to keep myself going. The voice attempted to persuade me once more, instructing me to find the knife, but I stuffed my fingers in my ears and started to hum through my tears.

Suddenly, as quickly as it had started, the pain ceased. As if someone had pressed a button, flicked a switch, it was over. Gasping, I sat up, tears still streaking down my face, my knees and hands coated in red clay. It had started to melt a little beneath me, and Aden caught my elbow when I tried to stand and slipped.

"Are you okay?" he asked, his black eyes appraising me as he started wiping the clay off my knees, my thighs, my forearms. I stood there, taking it, processing that I could, in fact, survive unspeakable acts of torture should I ever need to. Slowly, I wiped my tears away, straightened my shoulders, and nodded.

"Yeah. I'm good." The pain was gone. No amount of cautious movements in each limb produced even a twinge of discomfort. It was like it had never happened. "What now?"

We both jumped nearly a foot in the air when the altar started to quake and rumble. I darted behind Aden, having no qualms about using him as a djinn-shield, as the table, with its fine silk covering, sunk into the clay. When it disappeared, a rectangular opening sat in its place, with stairs leading down into the darkness.

"Three trials complete," Aden murmured, and I noticed a slight tremor in his words. "Down those stairs... sits an artifact that will change the world."

❦   *9*   ❦

"I CAN'T BELIEVE it's almost over," I said as we peered down the shadowy stairwell, hands on my hips. "I kind of feel like that was too easy."

Apparently, I'd already forgotten the pain—a bit like some women who forget the agony of childbirth and call it a miraculous experience, or something equally unbelievable.

"Well, you've made the only *actual* wood we can knock on, disappear," Aden muttered. He then reached over and rapt his knuckles on my head. I batted his hand away with a scowl, which disappeared when he grinned impishly.

Honestly, this guy was going to try my last nerve, but at least he'd make me laugh while doing it.

The djinn stepped around to what would've been the shorter side of the rectangular altar table, then bowed low. "After you, blessed hybrid."

"Gross." Taking a deep breath, I figured it only made sense that I should lead him into the final catacomb. So, I took the first step, my foot colliding with unyielding stone—a nice change from the somewhat melty, red clay. When no boobytraps triggered, I moved a few steps down. At the sound of Aden's grunt, I looked back, an eyebrow arched. "What's up?"

"I can't seem to…" He crouched down and smoothed his hands over the opening, then tried to push down. Something rippled in the air, like he'd pushed against a ward. To me, there was no resistance. I was able to walk out and back in unhindered, but Aden was unable to follow.

"I guess I'm doing this one by myself," I said, my heart sinking at the thought. Not that Aden had been much help on any of the trials, but I appreciated the silent emotional support. And, if I had to praise him, I'd say he'd been kind of, sort of… there for me when I wanted to stab myself in the heart with a silver dagger.

"I'll be right here if you need me," he insisted tightly as he knelt in the clay, his hands shimmering blue. I was about to ask how he intended to help me if he couldn't get through the wards, but the hands suggested there was more to his ability than I would ever know. With a stiff nod, I turned and carried on down the stairs, my hands out against the stone walls as I descended into darkness. When I reached the bottom of the stairwell, I glanced up and found Aden peering down at me. I raised a hand to my forehead, and he mirrored the salute.

Okay. I could do this. Whatever was left, it couldn't be worse than what I had just gone through—right?

Slowly, I moved into the pitch-black tunnel before me, and once I was far enough from the stairs, it was so dark that I couldn't see my own hand waving in front of my face. In no mood to go through this thing blindly, I called upon my illumination abilities. Slowly, my palms started to glow, and I tempered the harsh brightness with a warm yellow color. Finding that I no longer had to squint, I carried on.

The tunnel I found myself in was tall and narrow. Winding, it almost seemed to curve around the innards of the hill I'd completed the third trial on. Water dripped at a constant rate somewhere unseen, and the cool, dry air made my breathing almost *too* good. Slowing my inhales and exhales, I made each breath count. Purposeful. Precise. There was no telling if the original hybrids had tainted the air with one last defense mechanism.

But, all things considered, I'd think they'd make this a little easier. After all, only a hybrid could get through their trials. Technically, I was one of *them*. No hybrid out there would align themselves with someone like Jasmine, so, really, my mixed species background should've given me an express pass to the inner sanctum holding the artifact.

It felt like I'd been walking forever, and slowly, I realized the hairs weren't rising across my skin because of the drop in temperature. I whirled around quickly, hoping to catch whatever creature was staring at me, but found nothing but dead air and tunnel.

"Hello?" Probably the last thing I should say when I suspected I was being stalked, because now knew I was onto them. It might spur whoever it was into action. I waited, holding my breath, but was met with nothing more than the ever-present *drip, drip, drip* of a leaky tap. Shaking my head, I pushed onward, picking up my pace and hoping that Aden's promise of being there to help if I needed him, was real.

Finally, after an eternity of walking, I reached the end of the tunnel. Pausing, I shone my illuminated hands into the room, taking it in slowly. About three feet lower than the tunnel, it was the smallest room yet. Smooth marble lined the floors, ceiling, and walls. The only window, a skylight, allowed a single beam of unfettered moonlight to shimmer down on a pedestal, upon which sat two identical objects. With nothing else in the room, I could only assume one had to be this famed artifact.

Rather than waltzing right up to the pedestal and grabbing an artifact like the moron Aden assumed I was, I yanked off my shoe and tossed it into the room. When it hit the ground, I crouched and threw up whatever magical defenses I could. If this was the final test, one last trial that no one knew about, I imagined that the room might be rigged. However, when nothing fell from the ceiling or shot out from the walls or floor, I assumed it was safe to enter.

Slowly, I made my way across the room, grabbing my shoe and shoving it back on my foot along the way. I stopped at the pedestal. Two artifacts. Identical. Aden hadn't said anything about two artifacts. I frowned. Maybe he didn't know. Was the choice between them my true and final trial?

"Fuck me," I muttered. Each artifact could fit neatly in the palm of my hand. Small, round, smooth—there appeared to be a dip in the middle of the polished onyx, as if something went in there. On closer inspection, I noted a tiny tear in the center, too miniscule for a key, but noticeable to my enhanced sight.

Swallowing hard, I cautiously picked up the artifact on the left. Silence blanketed the dark marble room. It weighed more than it looked, and my skin erupted in goosebumps at the hum of its power. Like djinns, there was more to this little circle of onyx than met the eye.

While I trusted Aden to an extent, it wasn't like we were the best of pals, even after all of this. So, until I could figure out what the second artifact was for, I slipped it into my bra, sequestered safely on the underside, near the wire.

The moment I gently lifted the other artifact, shit decided to hit the fan. The room began to quiver and quake, and I sprang into action when a chunk of the ceiling crashed down into the floor.

Finally, a trap had been sprung—and I wasn't sticking around to see the aftermath. With a powerful burst of fae speed, I was out of the inner sanctum like a shot. In the distance, the distinct sound of Aden's screams filled my ears.

❧ 10 ❧

"WHAT DID YOU DO?" Aden snarled as I came racing up the stairs and back into the red clay room of the third trial.

"I got the fucking artifact, you psycho," I snapped. The chamber below continued to rumble, and as I'd zipped through at fae speed, the walls had started thundering down around me. A quick look back showed the stairwell collapsing in on itself. Meanwhile, all the red clay around us was starting to melt. A humidity gripped the room that hadn't been there before. Even the altar hill appeared shorter.

"Give it to me," Aden ordered, but I darted out of the way and slid down the hill.

"Not until we're out of here," I fired back over my shoulder. I knew that if he really wanted to, the djinn could overpower me magically, but I had an ace up my sleeve: the second artifact. Maybe both were needed for the full effect. Maybe one was a decoy. There were endless possibilities as to why there were two identical artifacts, and for now, I was keeping all my theories to myself. All that mattered was getting the hell out of there before we drowned in red clay.

Unfortunately, all hopes of a speedy exit came to a screeching halt when we discovered the doorway we had used to enter the chamber was now sealed shut.

"When did this happen?" I demanded, racing forward and slamming my fists against it. Slowly, clay dribbled down the wall like oozing lava, and I stumbled back before it covered my arms. Magic did neither of us any good—just as it had been with the boulder, our powers appeared ineffective against whatever the hybrids had concocted.

"I don't understand. We've completed the trials. This shouldn't be happening," Aden growled before hurling a blast of blue-black magic at the door. The room trembled, but nothing opened. Sweat ran down our faces as the humidity spiked, making it more than a little difficult to draw a deep breath.

"Well, it is." I scanned the room, then squinted up at the ceiling. Still black. Still too high to make out whether that would be a viable exit or not. "Let's just figure out how to get out of here."

"Now would be the ideal time to sprout a pair of *wings*, dragon shifter," he muttered, stalking by me and sloshing through the clay pooling at our feet.

I bit my tongue, stopping the snarky response I had in mind for him. I *couldn't* shift. The added stress and pressure of this situation wasn't going to somehow make it magically happen. There was no point in even discussing it—but of course he'd mention it now, just to crank up my guilt an extra few notches.

Huffing, I high-kneed my way through the clay, ignoring all thoughts of our impending death by red clay drowning. When my foot caught in something, I stumbled forward. Then I turned back and found my foot snagged in what looked like a handle.

"Aden," I called, crouching down. A quick blast of white magic temporarily cleared the clay, and I found myself staring at a hidden hatch in the floor. The djinn appeared by my side moments later.

"What?"

"Found our exit strategy," I grunted up at him. Yanking the

door open with all my might, I revealed a steep drop into nothingness.

"Yeah, I'm not going in there."

"Suit yourself," I insisted, skirting around the opening. "Stay here and wait for the rescue team that we both know isn't coming."

I met his dark gaze quickly, and when he stepped back and shook his head, I held up the artifact I'd had clutched in a death grip in my right hand. He gulped, but merely watched as I hopped down through the trap door, trusting that I'd land on my feet. After all, anywhere was better than the red clay room of humid death.

While I managed to land on my feet all right, it wasn't exactly solid ground I landed on. Knees bent, for the twenty seconds I fell I prepared myself for a gentle, soft landing, one where I would spring up and spare my lower half the impact of the fall. All that went out the window when I plopped unceremoniously into water—cold, deep water. I went under immediately, but managed to find the bottom with my feet a few seconds later, still holding the artifact tightly in one hand while the other remained safely inside my bra. Pushing up, I breached the surface with a gasp. The choppy water came up to my shoulders. With everything pitch black around me, I called on my illumination, lighting the space with my left palm and sputtering out salty water.

I appeared to have fallen in an underground river of some sort, one that gently flowed in one direction, which suggested to me that there was an exit somewhere. Preferring to hop along rather than swim, I bounced through the frigid water, fighting the urge to chatter my teeth as clay poured down from the hatch and muddied the river.

Moments later, I heard a curt cry from Aden, followed by a huge splash, and the sound of the hatch slamming closed. I whipped around to find him grappling with the same shock I had only moments earlier, wiping the water from his face and gasping.

"Welcome," I said, grinning as I shone my palm in his direction. He glowered for a moment, the light reflecting off the light blue water, then front-crawled toward me.

"I don't think this is much better."

"Is this room steadily filling up with melting clay?"

"Well, no, but—"

"Then this is better," I snapped, turning away with a huff. "I'm sure this water goes somewhere."

"Wait, wait..." Aden grabbed my arm and wrenched it toward the wall—as if I were his own personal half-fae flashlight. I tried to wriggle free, but stopped when I realized what he'd noticed. While my gut instinct had been to classify what we fell into as a sewer leading to some sort of drain, I couldn't have been more wrong. The walls were covered in art akin to cave paintings, but incredibly intricate and stylized. Color. Vibrancy. Little details like the ripples in cloth and wrinkles in skin. We inched closer, studying the art as a pair. This wasn't a sewer at all. It was a passageway that must have flooded at some point.

"It looks like a battle," I noted. Armies appeared to be meeting head on across green hills, banners flying high, swords drawn, beasts of all kinds in the mix. The figure dividing the opposing sides was a woman, her gown a beautiful cerulean to match her wild eyes.

"She's a hybrid," Aden whispered as he continued on without me, eyes wide and hands reaching out to touch her. "They all are..."

While the soldiers were a little more difficult to discern, the djinn wasn't wrong about our main girl. Wings like an eagle popped out of her back, yet she bore traditional elvish features everywhere else. In one hand she gripped a spear, the orange-yellow hue the most vibrant of the lot, and in the other she held a white shield. She wore a grim expression, like she stood between the battling armies because she had to, not because she wanted to.

I called Aden's name, then waded through the water to grab his arm when he ignored me. The djinn's fascination with hybrid lore would keep us here all night if we let it. I wanted to get out; the weight of both artifacts bore down on me more than I cared to admit.

"But…"

"You can come back later if you want," I argued, tugging him away, my body wracked with shivers. "We need to get out of here before we both catch hypothermia."

"I am impervious to human ailments—"

"Maybe I just want the pleasure of your company," I fired back with an annoyed sigh.

His snort made me grin—barely.

I GROANED SOFTLY, MY CHIN RESTING ON ADEN'S SHOULDERS. "We're going in circles. This is like the eighth time I've seen that painting."

"Oh, are we?" He stopped abruptly, the flood water sloshing against his knees. "Would you like to get off my back and give it a go? Does being part dragon mean you've acquired an exceptional sense of direction in this never-ending maze?"

Huffing, I shook my head. "No."

"Good. Then stop complaining."

"You… stop complaining," I countered weakly. Okay, so it wasn't my best banter, but I felt like absolute crap and was desperate for the sunlight.

We had been down here for hours, navigating the underground tunnels with nothing but one of my hands illuminated to guide us. I hadn't the strength for both. Once we cleared the shoulder-deep waters, I realized the trace amounts of iron present had sliced my energy in half. Barely able to keep up with Aden's most leisurely pace, he had offered me the opportunity of a lifetime: a piggyback ride on a djinn. At first, I'd refused, insisting that I could carry on without his help, but my knees kept buckling, my eyes wanted to close, and my stomach refused to stop churning. The iron present hadn't been enough to incapacitate me, but I'd suddenly felt like I'd been smacked upside the head with the flu, but without the snot and phlegm.

So, forgoing my dignity, I'd climbed onto to Aden's back, but only after he tugged off his trench coat and wrapped it around my shoulders.

"You're shivering," he'd said. While his tone had suggested he didn't care, back then I'd noted that he wouldn't look away until I put the coat on properly. Something in the fabric made it quick-drying, and soon enough I was warm enough to stop shivering. So, as much as I hadn't wanted to give him props for anything, the djinn certainly knew how to step up when I found myself floundering.

Aden waited for a moment, eyebrows lifted, as if giving me the opportunity to try that comeback again. I motioned weakly for him to continue, and he complied, trudging along through the now murky waters with me on his back.

"Have you still got it?"

I rolled my eyes. "The fucking artifact? *Yes*, just like I still had it when you asked five minutes ago."

"Confirm it."

"Oh my god, Aden—"

"Just do it," he insisted. "It's the only thing keeping me sane here."

Sighing, I fished the one artifact he knew about out of my coat pocket, then held it in front of him. "See?"

"Good."

I slid it back into my pocket, then, under the guise of readjusting myself, pressed my chest against his back. The slight pressure confirmed the other artifact was still hidden in my bra.

"While I love the feel of your boobs on my back," he said slyly, "you're making yourself heavier."

"Oh. Sorry." Cheeks red, I repositioned myself so that I was farther up on his back. "Better?"

"Yes."

"Just trying to get comfy."

"What a luxury," Aden sneered. "Comfort."

"Ugh, shut up."

He jostled me around, and I snapped my arms tighter around his neck, but when I caught his grin, I knew he wasn't serious about bucking me off—yet.

We carried on in an easy silence, ignoring the scratching sounds emanating from inside the walls. They had first popped up after we left the main tunnel with its deeper water, and they hadn't let up yet. Something with thick, large claws was trailing after us, and as I glanced back, scanning the area with my enhanced sight, I felt Aden quicken his stride.

Sometime later, in a new, tight tunnel that forced Aden to crouch, something on the wall caught my attention—and for once, it wasn't a painting.

"A ladder!" I all but shrieked in surprise, and Aden winced, my mouth right next to his ear. "Sorry... *Look!*"

Sure enough, rungs of a ladder stuck out of the wall. Aden shuffled over, and we peered up a long, vertical tube cut into the earth, the rungs leading all the way to the top.

"Is that sunlight?"

"It's some kind of light," Aden said, his vigor renewed. A halo of light glowed at the very top of the ladder. "And we're going to see where it takes us."

He slowly lowered me off his back, and I grimaced as my feet went back into the water. While I'd been feeling better—tired, but better—my head swam with that icky full feeling that came at the start of any bad cold. Congestion. It hit fast.

"D-Don't make me wait here," I said before I could stop myself. My inner voice concurred with nothing more than a grunt. The iron must have made it difficult to hear her, because she'd been silent for hours now. Aden tugged on one of the rungs, then shook his head.

"You'll climb up first." As I drew a breath to argue, he shot me one of his famous unimpressed looks. "So that I can catch you if you fall, you dolt. I'll be right behind."

Hmm. I could handle that. Unfortunately, I wasn't quite as confident in my hands' ability to grip things in that moment.

"There we go, out of the water," Aden murmured, his tone surprisingly patient as he lifted me, keeping a hand on my lower back. With his support, I managed to climb the first rung. Just as I'd suspected, I didn't have the grip strength right away. Eyes closed, I channeled whatever white magic reserves I could, fueling the power through my body. Only then could I lift myself up, one rung at a time, and truly begin to climb.

As promised, Aden was only a few rungs behind me. Although I could hear his huff of annoyance whenever I had to stop and catch my breath, he didn't sneer one awful word at me. Instead, he just waited, leaning back and sometimes asking if I was all right. It was the first time he had been so considerate of me, and I wasn't sure how to handle him when he wasn't wisecracking or calling me an idiot.

At the very top of the ladder, the portion circled in light seemed like a giant rock, with its edges rippled and sharp. Who used a rock as a manhole cover? Only in Alfheim. I tried at first to push it out of the way with one hand, then two, then squealed and clung to the ladder when I nearly lost my balance.

"Aden?"

"Hold on, give me a second," he grumbled. Then, out of nowhere, he climbed up the rest of the rungs so that we were pressed together, my back to his front. I could feel each of his strained breaths on my neck, and I pressed myself closer to the ladder, uncomfortable to be in such confined, intimate quarters with the djinn.

With us squished together, we took up the width of the

vertical corridor. Over my shoulder, I spied him leaning back against the wall, able to free up both hands without falling so he could shove at the rock covering. Thirty seconds later, with a gentle burst of magic from Aden, we were free.

Heart pounding, I scrambled up and out, flopping onto lush green grass at the base of a tree. Just as I'd suspected, someone had actually used a large rock to cover up the opening to the underground world, and I made a note to put it back once we decided our next steps. As I stared up at a beautifully blue sky, a warm gentle breeze washing over me, I was grateful to finally be free of that iron-soaked hellhole—its beautiful artwork aside. I knew we needed to get to Darius immediately. The artifact needed to be implemented ASAP—however it worked. Although it radiated power and magic, I wasn't sure how to activate it.

"Oh, I've never been so happy to see trees," Aden declared, contorting himself this way and that, as if to stretch out stiff limbs—only I'd never seen someone do a perfect ninety-degree angle mid-spine before. "This... This is perfect."

"Couldn't agree more." Based on how beautiful and serene everything was, I had to assume we were in elven territory. The sun appeared to have recently risen, yet I wasn't hungry. Something in the magical air down there must have sustained me.

Or maybe I was in shock, and all my bodily needs would hit me *hard* in about two minutes.

"Do you have the artifact?" Aden asked, that growly edge back in his voice that made the hairs on the back of my neck stand up.

"Same as before," I muttered, rubbing my eyes, *"yes."*

"Confirm it."

I groaned. All I wanted to do, for just a few minutes, was rest, breathe, and regather my strength. Instead, I peered up when Aden's shadow crossed over my face, and I found him standing almost directly on top of me.

"Fine." With some effort, I pushed up and onto my feet. My

whole body trembled, recovering from the prolonged exposure to even the bare minimum of iron, but I had the strength to dig the artifact Aden knew of out of my pocket and show it to him. "There, you, paranoid weirdo. Still got it."

"Good." His dark gaze flitted from the artifact to my eyes. "Very good."

My quip died on the tip of my tongue when he lashed out so fast that his hand was a blur, and clamped down on my wrist, yanking me toward him.

"What are you...?"

A strangled gasp crawled up my throat as black ice crept slowly through my veins, and I shot him one last incredulous look before my knees buckled.

Poisoned. Again.

The world clouded as Aden slowly lowered me to the ground, his expression grim. Although I was fading fast, I made sure to stare up at him for as long as possible. Let him remember his betrayal, the look in my eyes after all we had just been through.

Bastard.

And then, as I felt him brush the hair from my face, I finally succumbed to darkness.

❧ 11 ❧

I AWOKE WITH A GASP, eyes wide and chest heaving, feeling as though this wasn't the first time I'd done so since Aden wrapped his hand around my wrist and infected me. A third djinn poisoning, and I once again lived to tell the tale.

I was a freakin' miracle.

"Kaye," a familiar voice whispered as I tried to focus on the dimly lit room. My limbs felt stiff and aching despite the downy softness of the bed I found myself in, but my mind was steadily clearing. Seconds later, Zayne's worried face slid into view, and before he could say another word, I threw my arms around him and squeezed with all my might.

"Zayne!"

Somehow, I was safe, with family, and after a quick glance at my veins, no longer infected with the djinn's poison. My half-brother hugged me tightly, hushing me when the tears surfaced and fell. After all I'd been through, I couldn't stop the storm from quaking, the dams from bursting, and he just held me as I sobbed into his chest. A hand rubbed up and down my back, and when the flood finally eased, I managed to spare a peek over his shoulder and quickly realized I was in my old bedroom at the Hive.

"W-What?" I sat back with a sniffle, unshed tears still clinging to my lashes. The room seemed almost untouched since I had last used it, yet I couldn't understand how or why I was here. My last memory, besides the hazy bits of fog and gray that made no sense, was the forest. And Aden. And...

The artifact! I patted myself down, praying he hadn't found the spare, but Zayne gently took hold of my hands and held them within his own—his long fingers acting like snares.

"Take a breath," he instructed. "You're safe now."

"Zayne, I—"

"I had heard whispers that the dragon shifters were searching for you," he admitted, his brow furrowed, "but I didn't believe it. I assumed Darius would have come to me..."

"He... has a lot on his plate," I offered weakly.

"A few of my men found you wrapped in a trench coat at the edge of the city. We brought you to the Hive to heal in peace," Zayne told me with a slight shake of his head. "You've been in and out of conscious for about a day and a half now. It appeared you'd been poisoned by—"

"A djinn." I cleared my throat, in need of water. As if reading my mind, Zayne fetched a cool glass from the wooden desk beneath the window. I took a much-needed gulp, then another, and another, until I drained the cup dry and handed it back. A vision of Aden's face flashed across my mind, and I swore I heard my inner voice snarl. *The feeling was mutual, sweetheart.* "I know about the djinn. I remember. He kidnapped me."

Zayne's features contorted from tempered curiosity to flushed rage. "*What?*"

Before he flew off the handle, I composed myself as best I could and explained what I remembered about Jasmine's plan, the danger Darius's clan was in, and an asshole djinn named Aden. To his credit, Zayne listened to the whole story without interrupting once, though from the myriad of irate expressions dancing across his face, I knew he wanted to. Once I finished spilling all that happened over the last week or so, he stood stiffly and stalked out of the room.

In his absence, I checked myself over. No lasting wounds, and besides the foggy head, no lingering side effects of the djinn poison. He must not have given me much if I'd only been out for a day and a bit.

Clearly, Aden had double-crossed me and taken the artifact, but things seemed just a bit brighter when I found my belongings arranged in an orderly fashion on the bedside table. My waterlogged wristwatch. My clothes—cleaned and dried.

And the second artifact that had been hiding in my bra.

Unable to believe my eyes, I snatched it up and hid it under the covers, as if Aden might be lurking in the shadows, ready to steal it. With djinns, I couldn't be too cautious. I'd learned that now—and it was a lesson I'd never forget.

Zayne returned after I'd downed my third cup of water. Slowly, I was starting to feel like myself again and in *desperate* need of something fatty and fried. The artifact sat nestled in the pocket of the shapeless calf-length shift dress I'd been put in, resembling a hospital gown, but somehow even less flattering.

"I've ordered the men to mobilize," he told me, his tone curt —official, like he was still wearing his commander's cap. "We'll join the fight against Jasmine. The Sanctius clan will not fight her alone, whether that djinn gave her the artifact or not."

"We're going to Darius?" I asked, standing so fast the room spun. Balance lost, I scrambled for something to hold on to, only to have Zayne by my side seconds later, steadying me.

"Tomorrow," he insisted firmly, "when I'm sure you're ready, we'll go. The healers still have some work to do with you now that you're awake."

I smiled up at him as he lowered me into a chair. There was nothing quite like protective, brotherly love. Before, I'd always found it frustrating, maybe a little unnecessary. Right now, however, I wanted nothing else. "I love you, big brother of mine."

"And I love you, wild and reckless little sister of mine, even if you're going to turn me gray well before my time," he countered. Exhaling softly, he pressed a kiss to my forehead, then pulled up a chair beside mine. "Now, tell me everything about this djinn. Leave no detail out. I'll have him in the mind of every official in Alfheim, and all its bounty hunters, before sundown…"

IT NEVER CEASED TO AMAZE ME JUST HOW QUICKLY ZAYNE could summon his troops. After another day of healing in the Hive—the healers had requested more time, but I put my foot down, insisting we leave for the Sanctius clan *now*—I had followed my older, half-brother out of the underground world and into Alfheim proper. Standing at the portals was an impressive militia, considering he'd taken only a day or so to organize it. Following at his heels, I felt an ever-present sense of nostalgia clinging to me, like we had all done this song and dance before. This time, however, my dragon's clan was the prime target. Jasmine had sent assassins after me to hurt *him*. Before, the threat of Abramelin had loomed, but he was an elusive creature who none of us knew fully.

Jasmine, on the other hand, was someone I knew. I knew she was an impatient, uppity fae who would take her uncle's death and his army's defeat personally. She'd be pissed that I hadn't died. Vengeance was her middle name, and Darius was her target.

With surprising efficiency and Zayne at the helm, we all crossed through the portals leading back to Earth, leaving a swiftly recovering Alfheim behind us. From there, the militia portal-jumped in groups, eventually bringing us to the foothills of the Sanctius clan.

When we arrived, it was a very different village than what I remembered. Windows and doors on the lower halls were boarded up. Flags and banners had disappeared from the steeped roofs. The laughter of children around the schoolhouse was gone, and as I lead the first wave of Zayne's militia up the path toward the alpha's hall, I couldn't help but feel as though the village had died in my absence. The lack of bright, smiling faces. The lack of curious stares and whispers. All of it—gone. The slate gray of the mountainscape around us seemed enhanced, which only served to make the winding road up the steep incline even more desolate.

By the time we'd nearly reached the top, a dragon's roar thundered across the sky, harsh and powerful, like the crack of a storm's first thunder. The gray cloud cover above shielded the shifter tailing us, but every so often I spied his or her outline, puffs of gray dispersed with the grand flap of both wings. The supernatural beings behind me, many new and unfamiliar, cowered at the enormous presence, but I pressed on, climbing harder, faster, determined to find an answer for the state of the village where even the herb gardens seemed despondent.

A harsh wind whipped over us when we crested the final hill, reaching the top of the mountain just as a new group of the militia began to climb from the bottom. I looked back, scanning the landscape for unseen dangers. While there were captains and other ranks littered throughout the groups, I had offered to take the helm while Zayne decided to bring up the rear. No one would get left behind, and I refused to lead anyone astray.

When I was sure the others were safe, I told the group with me to wait. Darius's personal hall, the one I'd stumbled out of in a dream-like stupor under Aden's influence, was also boarded up. I swallowed hard, fighting back tears. He wouldn't have left. The clan wouldn't have abandoned their ancestral home, not even with the threat of Jasmine over their heads.

Suddenly, my inner voice uttered something between a squeal of delight and a long, forlorn moan. I winced at her volume, then whirled around and found the reason. A figure stood in the now open doorway of the alpha's hall, the only structure without planks of wood across its door. I drew in a soft breath, the outline instantly familiar.

Darius. Tears blurred my vision before I could even *think* of holding them back. For a moment, I forgot about the impending war, the militia, and Aden's betrayal. As I raced across the mountaintop, headed straight for my dragon's open arms, the only thing on my mind was him.

That I loved him.

That I wanted to marry him.

And that I was ready to be his mate.

"Darius!"

I slammed into him with such force that he actually stumbled back, but he didn't falter. I'd caught the jumbled emotions in those stormy gray eyes fleetingly, but I felt them in the way he held me. Our bodies melded together, the sturdy hard lines of his muscular form and my less than their usual voluptuous curves fitting against one another. Like the only two pieces of a puzzle crafted by fate and destiny. I hugged him hard, shaking, and I felt him slide his fingers through my loose red waves before breathing me in deeply, his nose trailing along my neck.

"Fuck, Kaye," he growled, fingertips digging into me as he hugged me tighter. "Don't you *ever* do that to me again."

"The next time a djinn kidnaps me, I *promise,* I'll let you be the white knight to my captured princess," I teased, though my voice quaked with emotion. "I promise, I'll consider a rescue."

He chuckled thickly, his coarse stubble scratching across my skin in the most delicious way. I suddenly found myself desperate for more physical contact, for fewer clothes between us, and no audience of supernaturals tastefully averting their gaze behind us. But as my hands wandered across the muscular planes of his torso, it was easy to forget averted stares and their lingering presence. All that mattered was Darius and me. Together. *Finally.* My fingers locked onto his black shirt and twisted the fabric. My breath hitched as his mouth trailed along my neck, turning an innocent caress into something darker, something tinged with barely restrained need that resonated deeply within me.

Teeth raked teasingly over my flesh, and I arched against him, my hands working their way into his wild hair as our lips met in a frenzied kiss. My desire for him spiked—the need burning fiercely inside, racing through my veins and pooling between my thighs. A soft moan slipped free before I could stop it, and Darius deepened the kiss with a growl, his tongue plundering my mouth, the act both possessive and desperate. Possessive before all others, marking me physically—the thought of which no longer frightened me. Desperate for closeness, our absence only thickened the invisible bond between us. Just the sight of him sparked a need in my very marrow, and from the way we touched one another, the way we kissed, it didn't take a genius to guess the one thing that might scratch this throbbing itch.

A pointed throat clearing behind me sucked some of the intensity out of the moment. Darius and I slowly untangled from one another's grasp. Smoothing my hair down, my cheeks flushed a telling crimson as I turned around. The fae behind me gave a half-hearted wave, his eyes dropping to the hand Darius still had resting on my hip.

"Galen?"

"Hi," my former second-in-command managed, clearing his throat before nodding back to the militia—which had swelled in size since I last looked. My blush worsened. *How long had we been kissing?*

"I didn't know you were traveling with us," I said, forcing the words out in an effort to break the awkward moment. To his credit, Darius appeared totally nonplussed that we were just sucking face in front of everyone. In fact, he looked, quite frankly, annoyed that we had had to stop.

"We haven't had a chance to say our hellos yet," he told me. "I'm just a regular soldier this time around, but I thought it might be prudent to, er, press pause on your reunion. Most of us have arrived."

"Bring them in through the hall," Darius instructed gruffly. "There is a door at the far back that will take you into the mountain. There will be someone to meet you when you arrive."

Galen nodded, then zipped back to the loitering supernaturals like the hounds of hell were at his heels. I smoothed my hands over my rumpled clothing, then tried to salvage my hair; Darius always brought out the wild creature within it. As we stepped to the side, nodding at a few supernaturals as they headed for the alpha's hall, I took a deep breath and squared my shoulders—but found that I couldn't shake my unquenched *need* for Darius. While I had always been interested in sleeping with him, touching him, kissing him, it was the physical attraction and emotional connection that encouraged my wanton thoughts. Now, as our fingers snaked around one another and I cuddled into his chest, I realized what I felt was rawer, more animalistic in nature.

Nature. That's what it was: the shifter part of me connected to him more firmly now, and the she-beast did *not* approve of this pause. The desire needed to be satiated, and *soon* if I wanted to form coherent thoughts, but I knew there were more pressing matters. Jasmine. Another war. The artifact. Fucking Aden.

Right. Back to business, I guess.

Take him, Kaye, my inner voice protested, but I rolled my eyes and ignored her.

"So..." I motioned in the direction of the village. "Care to tell me what's going on here? I thought you had all left from the way everything looks down there."

"That was intentional," Darius assured me, his thumb stroking the top of my hand in slow, even sweeps. When I glanced up, he appeared to be looking over the supernaturals entering his hall. There was more scrutiny in his eyes than the last time he had involved himself with the militia, but why wouldn't there be? This time, he was responsible for all the shifters in his clan. The weight of their lives rested heavily on his shoulders, and I found myself wanting to relieve him of some of the burden.

"To throw Jasmine off?"

"Quinn and Catriona were the first to spot her scouts," he said, scowling. "They were doing a sweep of the area with a patrol group and realized she had sent her uncle's old minions to spy on us."

"Did anyone get hurt?" Just thinking of Catriona being involved in all this made my heart hurt. My best friend had proven herself in battle and times of intense stress repeatedly in the past, but she wasn't meant for war. She was a delicate, graceful fae who had fallen for a dragon; they ought to be tucked away somewhere, exploring each other and falling deeper and deeper in love. That was all I wanted for her. Not this. "Catriona?"

"The only ones harmed were the spies," Darius stated, his tone curt. When he glanced down at me, his expression softened, and he kissed my temple. "Catriona is perfectly fine. She's waiting below. I moved everyone, including your father, brother, sister, and the Brisbane warriors, inside after we boarded up the village. There are many caverns and halls below ground that can be used in times of conflict. I'd hoped I would never need to fill them during my reign as alpha, but alas, here we are."

"Because of me." It slipped out before I could stop it, and when Darius's brow knitted in confusion, I cleared my throat and shrugged. "Jasmine wants to punish me, and she's doing that by targeting you. I killed her uncle. To her, *I'm* the abomination, more so than any whole shifter could be. The clan is in danger... because of me."

"Kaye, you know that isn't true."

I chuckled weakly. "It *is*. All of this is because of—"

"No." He tightened his hold on my hand and tugged me away from the hall. I noticed a few of the supernaturals watching us go, and just as I was about to argue that now wasn't the time to debate this, he silenced me with a swift kiss that stole my breath away. When he pulled back, he sighed softly and cupped my cheek. "Kaye, this would have happened with or without you. People like Jasmine... They just need a trigger. *Any* trigger. Yes, she could very well be focusing her wrath on me because of you, but don't forget... I actually dated that cretin. This could easily be a bit of post-relationship bullshit over some slight wrong that I don't even remember."

"I wouldn't put it passed her to do something like that," I muttered after considering it for a moment. Jasmine *was* petty enough to hold a grudge for this long. Darius grinned.

"See? It doesn't do anyone any good by placing blame. All we can do is prepare for what's to come. All we can do is react," he shook his head, "and survive."

Giving his hand a squeeze, I cocked my head to the side and appraised him. "When did you get so calm, cool, and collected?"

"When I suddenly had a whole village to take care of," he said with a chuckle. "If I lose my shit, they lose their shit. I don't think I've ever been this level-headed in my life."

"I knew you'd do it," I told him. "You know... Totally kill it as alpha. You've always had it in you."

"Well, we can't know that until Jasmine is dealt with," Darius muttered darkly, his gaze drifting back to the band of supernatural fighters filtering into his hall. "Any idea where she is?"

"Unless Zayne knows and hasn't told me, no." I bit my lip as I searched my brother out, then sighed. "I should try to track her down. Aden and the artifact... All of it traces back to me."

"Kaye, we've been over this."

"That doesn't change the fact that I need to find her," I argued, but something in his eyes, a perfect mirror of the heavy, humid clouds overhead, told me he wasn't about to back down. "Darius, I owe the clan—"

"We'll find her together," he told me. *Together, or not at all.* He didn't have to say it for the words to rattle around my skull. Of course, he would use that against me. Clever bastard.

"You can't leave the clan now."

"We're as safe as we'll ever be," Darius insisted. "Catriona has placed wards within the mountain itself. If Jasmine thinks we've left, then she won't come here. You and I can locate her within a few hours."

My eyebrows shot up. "Oh really? And how do you plan to do that? She could be literally anywhere... in any *realm*."

"Ravena."

I made a face at the mention of Darius's witch ex-girlfriend, the one who had stolen his wings with a vengeful curse—but then assisted us in tracking down my gargoyle assailants back when this whole journey began. It seemed like so long ago, like a full year had passed, when, really, I had stumbled upon a certain dragon shifter in a cave at the start of the summer. The hot weather was now drawing to a close, and fall was on the horizon. The season of the witch.

"Darius, I don't—"

"Ravena can use her mirror to locate just about anyone," he reasoned. "Look, I know she's not your favorite person, and you can damn well bet, she isn't mine, but if she can help, why not ask?"

"Because it could be a waste of time."

"It's our best hope at finding Jasmine. You know that."

I pursed my lips. He was right, after all. Even if she wasn't the warmest person around, Ravena had magical gifts the rest of us could only hope to learn after a lifetime of study.

"We'll see if there are any witches in the militia first," I said stiffly. Perhaps one of them could cast an equally powerful loca-tion spell. I didn't want to appear bitter about Ravena. After all, jealousy over Darius's exes was kind of pointless: Ravena stole his wings, and Jasmine was a homicidal manic. Nothing to be jealous about. Still, I would have preferred not to fall back on the witch as often as we did.

And twice was too often in my books.

"If they can't do it, we'll go to Ravena tomorrow morning," he told me. "No delays. No searching for an alternative."

"Deal." We shifted our clasped hands so that they formed a perfectly civilized handshake. When Darius gripped tighter, I responded in kind, and soon we had devolved into some silly thumb war like we were six. Zayne's voice, clear and crisp as he called out for me, broke the rare moment—the only one we'd probably get—and we eased apart.

"I should talk to him," Darius said, pressing a quick peck to my cheek before marching over to greet my half-brother. I watched him go, my head tilted slightly, and noted that in our time apart, he had changed the way he walked. He stood taller now, held his head higher, marched briskly and assuredly—confident. The Darius I had first met lacked confidence in many areas of his life, despite all his snarky bravado. But here, as he strode forth to greet Zayne, he moved with all the grace and poise of a true alpha.

I smiled to myself. A genuine dragon king.

$\approx$ 12 $\approx$

"THIS IS A MOST UNEXPECTED, and dare I say, *unwelcome* visit." Ravena stood in the threshold of her front door of the same run-down, backwoods mansion Darius had first brought me to when we needed her help. Decked out in black and purple lace, she stared down her thin nose at us. Much to my surprise, her mousey brown-blonde hair had been dyed since our last visit—to a startling shade of red. Almost the same shade as mine, actually. I glanced at Darius, wondering if that little detail had escaped him. Her eyes appeared even closer to emeralds than I remembered, and a nasty little voice at the back of my mind suggested she'd had them altered in Alfheim—so they would sparkle better than mine.

Which was absurd, and a touch paranoid on my part, but given how long the witch had pinned after my dragon, it wouldn't surprise me if she'd made a few alterations.

"Ravena, you know we wouldn't be here unless we really needed your help," Darius insisted, and I braced myself, knowing full-well that that was the absolute worst way to address a scorned ex. Her expression darkened, her lips momentarily pinched, so I took the opportunity to try to smooth things over before she slammed the door in our faces.

"You're the only one powerful enough to help," I clarified. "Please. We've been working with other witches, but none of them compare to you."

Her features brightened, swallowing the obvious flattery—flattery that wasn't an outright lie. Just as Darius had promised, we *did* work with the witches in the supernatural militia. Even Catriona and I had banded together—after a tearful reunion and a hug that lasted the better part of an hour, of course—to attempt a location spell together. After all, our combined knowledge of Jasmine beat out the others, who had tried magically tracking her based on wordplay and vague, all-encompassing spells. Catriona and I could actually visualize her properly. Together, we knew every detail of that horrible fae, right down to the way she always wore her nails—polished, long, ornate and pretentious.

The other witches had managed to locate Aden, working off his trench coat that he'd left me wrapped in after poisoning me. Apparently, he was sitting on his ass in a Brooklyn dive bar, looking rough and haggard. None of the witches were able to confirm or deny if he had the artifact on him, but he wasn't with Jasmine. At the time, I couldn't decide how that made me feel, but it didn't change my opinion of him. After we all agreed to let the djinn be for now, we refocused our efforts on Jasmine as a collective whole...

But we'd all failed. Not wanting to waste more time, I had conceded to Darius's plan to rely on Ravena and her black mirror which was enchanted to peer into the future *and* locate missing objects, among other things I was sure. We had spent the night portal hopping, then flew the rest of the way above the cloud cover. So, in that moment, not only was I sore from straddling Darius's enormous, spiky back for a few hours that morning, but I was also sleep-deprived and cranky. Not exactly the right mindset to go up and ask my man's ex-girlfriend for help, but I knew how to play this game better than Darius.

"I'll listen to your needs," Ravena remarked, the rush of irate color fading from her cheeks as she surveyed us, "and *consider* lending my assistance."

"Thank you," I said, taking a step up toward the huge doorway, following Darius's lead when Ravena inched aside. However, as soon as Darius was through the door, she held up a hand, blocking me.

"Darius can explain it without you, I'm sure," she insisted, then closed the door so fast that it actually hit the end of my nose. I staggered backwards down the steps, scowling. So much for getting us back on her good side. *Petty witch*. When I tried to listen in on the conversation inside, magnifying my hearing for the first time in a while, I was greeted by nothing more than a static buzz that made me dizzy. A low growl of discontentment and distrust rumbled in my mind. It seemed my inner dragon was certainly unhappy with this development.

Clearly, she had learned and adapted from our last visit. No hiding in the bushes and listening in on private conversations this time. I exhaled sharply, annoyed. Something magical kept me out, enhanced senses and all, so I settled on the edge of the front steps, arms crossed and eyes heavy, and waited.

If I didn't dislike her as much as I did, I might have asked what, exactly, she used to muzzle my abilities. It could certainly be useful in the fight against Jasmine if we could fully protect shifter communities to outside supernatural prying. Wards concealed and contained all that was inside from intruders, but many could still penetrate them with a skilled ear. It took a lot of talent to block all the senses.

Ten minutes—that felt like an eternity—later, I heard the front door unlocking. Sighing, I stood and found myself greeted by Darius, his expression a strange mix of frustration and relief.

Classic Ravena.

"She'll help us," he told me as he ushered me inside. I didn't bother to wipe the dust and dirt and dead leaves off my boots, but rather tracked them inside—because the inside of Ravena's mansion was the same as the outside, and both were in desperate need of a cleaning.

"She will? Why?"

"Apparently, she's a staunch supporter of your brother," he remarked. "She's stayed out of the fight so far, but wants to contribute to the effort."

My eyebrows shot up. "Well, color me surprised."

"That's how I feel too."

I wasn't surprised, however, that she hadn't offered her abilities to the war efforts in a bigger way. Ravena struck me as a homebody—dare I say a hermit, even. I didn't judge her for it; all that mattered now was that she was going to help us.

"I'll need a drop of blood," Ravena insisted as she strode back into the foyer, her black mirror in hand. I bristled at the potent pulse of iron, which made up the mirror's handle—something else that I didn't recall from our last visit. Emerald green eyes fixed on me. "I'll take it from you this time, hybrid."

Trying very hard not to roll my eyes, I extended a hand and let her prick the tip of my finger with a silver dagger hanging off her utility belt. She seemed to stab a little harder than necessary, but I refused to flinch under her scrutiny, and schooled my features before turning my hand over and letting three droplets of blood drip onto the black mirror's face. As soon as the last droplet landed, the mirror's surface changed, swirling in on itself like a whirlpool, and the three of us gathered around it, our reflections quickly distorted before disappearing completely.

Smoke wafted across the mirror's surface in soft, billowing curls. I tried not to inhale it, my experience with djinn tricks causing my heart to hammer, but it wasn't there for long. The mirror absorbed it, swallowed it back down, and suddenly the blackness disappeared—in its place, a woman.

"Jasmine!" I cried out, stunned that it had worked so quickly. The mirror focused in on her eyes, bright blue and cold, then panned out to the rest of her face. The sight of it, of her, made my stomach roil, and I glanced briefly at Darius, who wore his contempt in the clench of his jaw and the steeliness of his eyes. Smoke hugged the edges of the vision, never bringing it into full focus, but I recognized the setting—to an extent. Jasmine stood over a table, into which the chalk outlines of both Alfheim and the US were drawn. She leaned on the table, her hands curled around its edges, and scowled. Stars littered both maps, and I gasped softly when I realized what they were: shifter communities.

Aden hadn't lied about that. She *was* targeting them again. She had picked up her uncle's fallen banner and planned to succeed where he had failed.

Well.

There were going to be two monumental failures in that family if I had anything to say about it.

Behind her, the scenery was less clear. Muddled. Smoky.

"Can't you make it clearer?"

"The mirror shows what it wants to show," Ravena told me curtly. "I am but a conduit."

"It looks like she's in a tent," Darius muttered, twisting his head this way and that, as if to examine it from all angles. "Like... Like a general's tent on the battlefield."

Our eyes met as a thought occurred to me. "We might already be too late."

"Our scouts haven't detected anything like that in the area."

"She could have it enchanted."

Darius exhaled sharply, and while he looked on the verge of storming off, he stayed put and returned his gaze to mirror. "What is that?"

"What?"

"There..." He pointed to the right side, behind Jasmine's shoulder, and I peered more closely. The figure was small with delicate limbs and gentle features, albeit it was as unclear as the rest of the background of the scene. Only Jasmine was in full focus, but from what I could make out, it looked like a child.

Jasmine had no children. I seriously doubted it was hers.

So, what was it doing there?

I shook my head. "I don't... Is that...?"

"A child?"

"Are you sure you can't go closer," I asked Ravena, wondering if she was just screwing with us for kicks, but the glare she shot me suggested otherwise. Shrugging, I looked back to the mirror. It didn't matter why there was a child there, or if it was Jasmine's, or if it even *was* a child. All that mattered was finding her. "If she walks out of the tent, will the mirror follow her?"

"It will."

"Then we just have to wait for her to leave," I said, nodding. "We can't make heads or tails of anything while she's in there."

"Then we'll wait," Darius agreed. "I doubt it will take long. She's never been one to sit still."

"Or brood over a map making strategical decisions," I said with a smirk. Darius's little half-chuckle was enough to tell me the joke had landed where it needed to. Still, I couldn't shake the shadowy figure behind her, its features dancing in and out of focus, and I swore I saw ropes wrapped around it, just below the shoulders. A prisoner, maybe? "But this child..."

I set my fingertips on the edge of the mirror, an unconscious movement to bring it closer to me rather than me going to it, but the instant physical contact occurred, the image changed completely. Gone was Jasmine in her tent with her maps. Instead, I saw Darius.

Wounded.

Alone.

Blood trickling from a gash on his temple.

He crawled across a field slick with blood, his clothing tattered. Other broken bodies lay strewn around him, their faces obscured, but their pain palpable. I trembled, some magnetic pull forcing my fingers to remain on the mirror, forcing me to watch him suffer, crawling for something, someone, his cries incoherent but his despair evident. Tears blurred my vision. He was so alone.

And I...

I was nowhere to be seen—nowhere in this vision as my dragon lay dying, suffering, in his last moments.

As the first tear dribbled down my cheek, the connection broke. I yanked my hand away as though the mirror burned me, but before I could get a word out, a crippling static feeling shot through my body. My eyes widened. My body crumpled to the floor.

The last thing I remembered before I fainted completely was Darius shouting my name—and the feel of his strong arms catching me.

❧ 13 ❧

EVEN THOUGH I couldn't see the storm from within Darius's hall, I felt it. I lived it, sitting in front of the small fire in the hearth with my knees drawn to my chest and my eyes heavy. Rain hammered the boarded-up windows, cold and foreboding, a telling sign that summer was on its way out. Every few minutes, lightning struck, illuminating the few holes and gaps between the boards. I glance up, counting until the thunder cracked. They say every second was a mile away. That was where the heart of the storm was. The last flash of lightning had but two Mississippi counts before the thunder rumbled, seemingly right over the mountain range. Its raw power made the small hall shudder. I felt it in my bones.

At the sight of the fire settling, I added more kindling that Darius and I had collected before the rain started. Bits of twigs. Spiny, dry underbrush. The fire consumed them all within seconds, drawing life, drawing energy, in order to carry on crackling. I leaned in closer as the heat swelled, finding comfort in the warmth, enjoying the way it danced across my cheeks. The flames had lulled my inner voice to sleep a half hour ago, seeming to quiet her frantic chatter. If only it could do the same for me.

I couldn't shake the vision I'd seen in the mirror. Darius. Suffering. Dying. All alone in a field of blood and corpses. When I'd come to, courtesy of Ravena's potent smelling salts, I had learned that the black mirror *chose* who to give visions to. It went by physical touch, but, Ravena had noted, it responded primarily to the blood offering. I had provided three droplets of blood—and apparently, the mirror had something desperate to share, just waiting for me to connect with it as we searched for Jasmine.

Terrified, I had spent the rest of the afternoon sitting outside. While Darius hadn't wanted to leave me, I forced him to sit and watch the mirror, to follow Jasmine's movements. That was what mattered—not my vision. Unfortunately, as the hours had dragged on and Jasmine refused to leave her tent, we had decided to call it a day. Knowing that she was preparing for war was good enough, for the time being, and we returned to the Sanctius clan village the same way we had left it: portals and flying.

As if sensing I wouldn't do well sleeping at the makeshift camps within the belly of the mountain, Darius had told me we'd spend the night in his old hall. He removed some of the wood planks in order for us to get inside, but for the most part, it still looked abandoned. While I had protested the idea at first, wanting to be close to my family and Catriona, the vision of Darius's death plagued me well into the night. I hadn't been able to focus or contribute much to conversation, and in the end, separating myself from everyone to collect my thoughts had been the best approach.

But Darius was still alpha, so I had insisted he see to everyone inside before turning in for the night. As the sound of the doorknob rattling reached my ears, I figured he had finally returned. A quick look at the old ticking clock told me it was shortly after midnight.

"Fucking rain," Darius grumbled as he came staggering into the room, drenched and dripping. My lips twitched into a smile at the sight. Dragging his seemingly useless rain poncho off and hanging it on the hook behind the door, he met my eyes and scowled. "You'd think it was the end of the world with how it's coming down out there."

"Makes you wish we were inside the mountains, huh?" I winced at the morose quality of my voice. While the vision wasn't guaranteed to come true, I couldn't deny its effect on me. The thought of Darius dying... Well, that alone was enough to send me spiraling.

"Hardly," he remarked. "There's nowhere I'd rather be than right here with you."

I tore my gaze from the fire, my smile turning appreciative as he stripped out of his wet shirt and tossed it aside, followed quickly by his pants. Shadows flickered across his body, highlighting the toned curves of his chest, his thick shoulders, and the defined bam-bam-bam of his abs. How I'd ever managed to snag a man so sinfully sculpted was beyond me. Apparently, I'd done something *really* good in a past life, because the mere sight of him, with his skin glistening from the rain and his boxers clinging to his thighs—well, I finally understood the phrase *fire in her loins* that all the old romance novels went on about.

Strolling to the bed, he provided an ample view of an equally stunning backside and rippling muscles shifting along his back. He toweled off briefly with a blanket, then grabbed another and headed back for me. I returned my stare to the fire, flustered for a better reason than before. At least I knew the vision-induced funk didn't distract me from *everything*. Nothing like a perfect ass in clingy boxers to chase the blues away.

"How are you feeling?" he asked as he settled down beside me, wrapping the blanket around both of us. As his arm snaked around my waist, I shuffled in closer, curling up against his warm chest. My hand lazily wandered the muscular dips and curves. I grinned when he twitched as I passed over a known ticklish spot. "Kaye..."

"I'm... okay," I admitted softly after retreating a little, fiddling with the frayed edge of the blanket over my shoulders.

"I'm sorry I've been so out of it. That vision... It really shook me, I guess."

"I know." He slid a finger down my cheek, a whispered caress as the fire spit and hissed at us from the hearth. As if to appease it, I tossed in some more kindling, and while the flames grew higher, the tantrum ceased. After settling back against my dragon, I closed my eyes and listened to the steady beat of his heart, smiling when he kissed my forehead. "You know, what you see in that mirror isn't prophecy. It isn't guaranteed to happen. I don't think even Ravena understands the nuances of that thing. She claims to understand it, but I've always thought of her as more of a servant to a magical object's unyielding demands."

"Hmm." I hummed my acknowledgement, but even then, there was no way I could just forget what I had seen. No one ever wanted to see a loved one suffering so horribly. Whether it was prophecy or not, I was sure I'd have nightmares about it when I finally let sleep take me.

"Besides, we have to focus on Jasmine," he muttered after showering me with a few more pecks—my forehead, my temple, my cheek. Each one stoked the embers of desire within me, spurring that *particular* fire back to life with ease.

"We're preparing for an attack," I said with a slight shake of my head. "I don't know what else there *is* to do. If we can't find her, we're just sitting ducks until she graces us with her presence."

And that was *if* she ever attacked. After reconvening with Zayne when we returned to the village that evening, we had all considered the possibility that there was no attack, that Jasmine was just spreading rumors, falsifying her location, in order to send the shifter world back into chaotic scrambling. To incite fear. To push us into hiding. I wouldn't put it past her, of course, but I also told everyone that I thought her rage and her need for revenge—to come out on top—was stronger than her ability to play mind games. Catriona had backed me up on that. For now, we treated her as a very real threat, and preparations continued deep within the mountain in response.

Hogar had actually finalized a few dragon saddles, which would allow some of our supernatural fighters to fight in the sky if necessary.

"Well, even if my vision wasn't prophecy, our viewing of Jasmine was in real time," I said after a brief pause. One of Darius's hands wandered over my side, grazing my curves and smoothing along the dips in my body. Distracting as it was, I was able to *almost* ignore him. "If she has a child with her, a prisoner, we have to find them."

"We will."

"Yeah?" I glanced up at him. "And how do you know that? How are you so sure?"

"Because *together*, we can do anything," he rumbled, stealing a kiss from my lips this time, drawing my bottom one between his teeth ever so gently. My eyes fluttered closed as my head tipped back, his hot breath dancing across my sensitive skin. Desire coiled within my core. When he released me, I straightened up with a gulp, my heart racing.

"What is this, an after-school special?" I teased, though the breathy quality of my words took the sting out of the jab. He grinned, one of those knee-buckling, pulse-pounding, swoon-worthy grins, and it took everything I had within me not to pounce on him right then and there. "I do not approve of these underhanded tactics of distraction, Mr. Thomas. This is a serious conversation."

"Well, maybe I've just missed you, *Miss* Allister," he countered huskily, "and this is the first opportunity I've had to get my hands all over you without ten other people watching."

While I loved our banter, the reminder that I had been away —trapped, prisoner of a djinn courtesy of a fae psychopath—put a bit of a damper on things. As if sensing his mistake, Darius drew me in to his chest again, rubbing my back beneath the blanket.

"You know, we haven't really talked about what happened during the trials. Not in detail."

I swallowed hard. He was right, of course. I'd gone into some vague detail about what Aden and I had experienced while collecting the artifact, but we'd been so busy with everything else, that this was the first time we could actually *talk*. However, when I peered up at him, I found I didn't *want* to talk. I didn't want to share the fine details of each trial, because not only would it make him worry, it would make him feel guilty for having me go through it alone—especially the third trial.

"It doesn't matter what I had to do," I said softly, then gasped when Darius caught my chin and tilted my face up to his, our eyes seeking one another out.

"It matters to *me*, Kaye."

Licking my lips, I exhaled my surrender, a gentle concession to the fact that he had a right to know. However, as I tried to explain what had happened, I realized I couldn't find the words beyond stating that my strength, my wisdom, and my will were tested—thoroughly. And that I survived unscathed, until a certain djinn tricked me for the last time.

"Kaye... I know this is difficult, but—"

"All that matters," I said, raising my voice over the crash of thunder. This time, the pounding rattled the covered windows, feeling like a tiny earthquake pulsing through the longstanding mountain range. I took a moment to collect myself, my eyes swimming with tears before I could fight them. "All that matters, is that I came to a decision at the end of the third trial. It was the most intense of the three. The magic was there to break me, and as I fought, I realized... I realized that I didn't want to die. I wanted to live, to fight... to... to be your mate."

Darius's brow twitched upward slightly, his eyes boring deeply into mine. He took a moment, as if needing it to process my words, and when realization washed over him, I couldn't help but smile. Catching my lower lip between my teeth, my smile bloomed to match his, and I nodded, tipping my face up just as he leaned down, our mouths colliding together in a rush of passion that made my toes curl.

His tongue swept across my lips, and I happily parted them, allowing a dance of tongue and teeth to commence as I twined my fingers through his hair. Long, wild, wet—and all mine. My inner voice seemed to have called in the angelic choir, because I'd never *felt* her happiness quite like this before—while she said nothing at all. Pure silence. Yet her pleasure became mine, pumping hard through my veins with every touch, every caress of Darius's hands over my body. They roamed as though on a mission, cupping my breasts through my shirt, questing downward to curve over the swell of my backside. A little yelp slipped out when he hoisted me up with firm hands on each cheek, and hauled me onto his lap.

I sat straddling him, my hips writhing as if with a mind of their own, up and down his torso, tendrils of pleasure unfurling through my core. The soft groan caught in his throat suggested I wasn't the only one savoring the moment, and as his mouth left mine to press hot little nips along my jaw and down my neck, I felt him grow hard against my center.

"Darius," I whispered, my fingers digging into his shoulder and my eyes widening when he sucked hard on the sensitive skin where my neck and shoulder met, "I love you so much. I'm sorry I couldn't give you an answer before, but I know now... I can't imagine my life without you. I want to be your mate, your partner..."

I trailed off, moaning wantonly when he bucked beneath me, the bump of his hardness sending a jolt of pleasure through my body.

"My *everything*," he growled against my skin. "You are my everything."

The feel of his fingertips against my flesh, digging under my shirt, made my breath stutter, and I lifted my arms to oblige as he yanked my shirt off over my head. If I hadn't, I suspected he might have just torn it from my body, shredding it to pieces in his haste to touch me, *taste* me—and I wouldn't have had it any other way. The desperation for skin-to-skin contact—I understood it. I suffered from it, and had suppressed my desires for too long. For the sake of the war. For the militia. For our families.

No longer. It was time to *take*, to be selfish, to give in to those primal urges roaring to life within me.

"I need... more," he snarled as he dragged his mouth down my bare body, my bra a distant memory. I leaned back to give him better access, arching my back and tossing my head in wild abandon. His lips trailed across each creamy mound before closing over one pink, beaded pearl. The feel of his tongue, the hint of teeth, raking over the hardened bud sent a delicious combination of pain and pleasure coursing southbound—destination: the wetness between my thighs. I whimpered his name as he swept his thumb over the other bud, and he responded with another growl, rolling us over and onto the blanket.

"I need more, Kaye," he whispered, his voice a gravelly, husky mess that did wicked things to my mind and body. "I need all of you."

"Take it," I told him, lifting my hips when he thumbed the waistband of my black leggings. "All of me. It's yours."

"And I'm yours." He descended upon me with a savagery that should have frightened me, but as I bowed to his lips, my arms snaked tightly around him. All I wanted was *more*. More of him. More of us. More of everything.

Tearing his mouth from mine, he eased down my body again with a sudden agonizing slowness, the kind that made me twitch and whimper, pressing my lips together to contain the squeal as his tongue delved into my navel while his hands ripped my leggings down. Straightening up for a moment, he seemed to consider me, his greedy eyes drinking me in.

I love you.

I heard his voice in my head, and whether it was real or imagined, it made me smile as I tried to quiet my heaving breaths. In the past, I had always shied away from being totally bare before a new lover, but with Darius, there was no shame. No reason to hide. We belonged to each other.

My eyes drifted closed, and I shuddered as he lowered himself between my parted thighs. Each tantalizing kiss placed, almost strategically, along my thighs only served to torment me further, to rile me up again with no hope of release in sight. I whined softly, my hand shooting down to steer him where I most desperately needed him. But he ducked out of the way with a dark chuckle, the sound washing over me, his breath hot against my skin.

"Darius," I whimpered, my hips grinding down toward him. I caught him smirking as he peered up at me, his eyes darker than the storm clouds outside.

"Impatient, are you?"

"I can do it myself, you know, if you don't hurry up."

His smirk grew. "I very much doubt that, sweetheart."

Then, before I could get my retort in, his mouth captured the helm of my womanhood, and fireworks shot through me. I arched up, moaning, my eyes practically rolling back in my head as he teased me with his extremely talented tongue. Over and over, his ravished me with his attentions, positioning my legs over his shoulders for better access. Just as I was on the verge of a climax, my skin prickled with goosebumps and my muscles clenched, ready to fall off that cliff, he moved lower and speared me with his tongue. I cried out, bucking against him as his thumb picked up where his mouth had left off, rubbing me, tormenting me with wild abandon. His breath was like fire, lapping at my skin, washing over me with a crackling, spitting flame that the actual fire in the hearth was no match against.

He brought me to the edge and back, over and over again, delighting in my cries, and holding me still with one hand stretched up to cover my breasts. The unending thrust of his tongue, the relentless gentle flick of his thumb over my most sensitive spot—it was enough to drive me mad. But I eventually pitched forward instead, tumbling into the abyss with a smile on my face as a powerful climax took hold. With the might of a hurricane, it pounded through me, striking me blind, deaf, and dumb to the rest of the world—all except for *him*. Toes curled, I cried his name, riding out the pleasurable waves as he prolonged them with slow, tantalizing sweeps of his tongue.

As I slowly came back into my body, I felt Darius kissing his way up it, until eventually our lips met in a crash of unbridled need. While the climax had satisfied one craving, it had left another, far larger one, in its place. More. More. *More*. All of him, all of me—together, or not at all.

I swallowed my surprised cry when he slipped an arm under me and scooped me up. Still tasting myself on his lips, his tongue, I threaded my fingers into his beastly mane. A soft shudder slipped out when my back collided with the wall, and I wrapped my legs around his waist, ankles locked behind him, as I cupped his face and held him to me. If I could help it, I would never stop kissing Darius—not until we were both gasping for our very last breath. Outside, the storm raged on—rain hammering the hall so masterfully that I could almost feel each droplet through the stone.

For a moment, I almost wanted to be out in it. Right in the thick of things. Just me, my dragon, and the might of Mother Nature. I suspected our union, our moment, would outweigh hers any day.

"I love you, Kaye Allister," Darius hissed against my lips, reaching down to free himself from those gloriously clingy boxers. "And I will honor you as my mate, the woman the fates have aligned me with, until my dying day."

He smothered my words before they escaped with another kiss, his tongue thrusting between my lips in tandem with him pushing inside of me. I cried out, the sound swallowed between us, as he filled me, stretched me in all the right ways—made me feel whole for the first time in all my life. I tugged at his hair, desperate for him to move when he stilled inside of me, groaning as the renewed throb of slowly mounting pleasure began again inside me. Darius nipped at my lower lip in response, then snatched both of my wrists and pinned them back against the wall. I wrenched my lips free of his, grinning sinfully, ready to fight with the only strength I had in that moment: my words.

But he stole those away too, bucking hard against me before capturing my mouth once more. His thrusts grew harder, faster, more insistent, and all I could do was cling to him for the ride. My hands curled to fists as that little nugget of pleasure in my core tightened, twisted, and thrummed with the possibility of more. I'd feel it tomorrow, the bruising force of his hips pounding against mine, the crushing grip of his hands wrapped around my wrists—and I'd relish it. Savor it. Long for it again. I rocked up to meet him as best I could, sucking on his tongue, reminding him that I was my own dragon, my own fae—that I wouldn't be *conquered*, but cherished. He dominated our pace, taking me heatedly against the wall, but *I* controlled our kiss, my teeth snaring his bottom lip and drawing a satisfying growl from him.

We plummeted over the edge together this time, first Darius spilling himself into me, then me falling after as our hips ground together to prolong the ecstasy. Our breaths fell like thunder, but we held each other as if the world was ending. As I inhaled him, I tasted his fire, felt it course through me—felt it breathe life into me unlike anything I'd ever felt before. When our eyes met, his wild and dangerous, mine focused and captivated, I knew he felt it too.

Without a word, Darius hoisted me up suddenly, adjusting his grip, and carried me to the door. Before I could protest, he walked us outside, totally buck naked. Something mixed between a laugh and a cry jumped out of me at the feel of the first droplets of rain, quickly smothered by the thousands more. Cold. Revitalizing. Thunder rumbled in the distance after a bolt of lightning illuminated the sky.

"You think you have another round in you, sweetheart?"

Darius whispered in my ear. When I bit my lip and grinned, he chuckled. "I thought we could use a change of scenery."

"Fucking in the middle of a crazy summer storm? What kind of girl do you take me for?"

He smirked. "I take you for *my* girl..."

I blinked the rainwater from my eyes, so in love with him that it *hurt*, and kissed him.

❧ 14 ☙

I AWOKE to the feel of someone, or something, tapping my forehead. Either this was a very vivid dream, or Darius had a death wish. Groaning, keeping my eyes clenched shut, I swatted at whatever was harassing me—but hit nothing. The tapping stopped. Pleased, I snuggled deeper into the pillow, a pillow that smelled so strongly of Darius that it was like a drug. Beside me, my dragon's breathing hitched briefly, then quickly evened out.

It must have been nothing.

The lingering memory of a dream.

No dreams, Kaye. Right. I couldn't recall having dreams, even though I should have. After all Darius and I did last night, I *definitely* should have had some pretty awesome dreams, frankly. But in that moment, I remembered hitting the pillow after *six* amazing climaxes, both in and around Darius's mountaintop hall, and then it was black nothingness for the rest of the night.

Another *tap-tap-tap* in the center of my forehead. "Kaye?"

My eyes snapped open, the voice instantly recognizable, and I sucked in a panicked gasp at the sight of Aden's face about an inch from mine. The djinn's black eyebrows lifted, and his thin mouth curved into a smirk.

"G'morning, sleepyhead." He cocked his head to the side.

"That was like waking the dead... You two have a satisfying reunion?"

The wiggle of his eyebrows wasn't exactly subtle.

I swallowed hard, as my sluggishly sleepy mind tried to process whether this was a dream or a very cruel reality. My inner voice fired off alarm bells left, right, and center. Definitely real.

So, I responded with a scream—one that would certainly wake the dead. Aden scrambled back, his eyes wide as a huge, burly, naked figure leapt over me. Within seconds Darius had the djinn tackled to the ground.

And proceeded to kick the living crap out of him.

Well, kick was the wrong word—Darius was a fist man, it would appear. As I sat up with the blankets drawn up to hide my modesty, my body sore from last night's activities, I watched in both horror and satisfaction as my dragon pummeled the djinn into the ground.

I had to give it to Darius... He'd been asleep beside me only seconds earlier, and the fact that he could snap into action so fast was beyond impressive. Never would I have to fear an intruder breaking into our bedroom. Those lightning fast reflexes would take care of *anyone* who dared try.

"That's the djinn!" I shouted over the commotion. "The one who took me!"

"I know," Darius snarled, his face scrunched in rage, his fists still flying. "I remember him from the spell."

The militia witches had apparently produced an image of Darius while Catriona and I were working on locating Jasmine. From the way Darius manhandled Aden, I could only assume he'd been present for that feature film.

"Kaye," Aden barked, finally managing to block a few blows —though he didn't appear to be trying very hard. Maybe he thought he deserved a bit of a beating, which would serve him right. "Get your fucking *naked* mate off me!"

"Darius, try not to kill him," I mused as I held Aden's gaze, hoping mine looked as icy as it felt. "I'm sure all that blood will be hard to scrub off the floor."

"You know I could get out of this," the djinn fired back, and I straightened at the sight of his hand slowly succumbing to that blue djinn fog I'd seen before.

"Darius." I tried to keep the fear out of my voice, but I knew Aden was right. If he operated at even half his full capacity, the djinn could probably wipe the entire Sanctius clan off the map. No idea why their species ever restrained themselves. So much power. So much possibility. "Darius, stop."

"Just a few more hits," my dragon grunted, landing one right in the middle of Aden's face in his moment of distraction. At the sound of something crunching, or maybe cracking, followed shortly by Aden's cry of pain, Darius retreated. He loomed over the djinn, hands curled to fists, chest heaving. If looks could kill, Aden would have been six feet under by now, and when Darius glanced back at me for a split-second, even I feared him. "I caught his scent the second you screamed."

"Ever consider hiring yourself out as a bloodhound?" Aden sat up slowly, dark purple blood splattered across his face. He fiddled with his nose, squishing it between his fingers. I wrinkled my face at the sound of broken cartilage and bone being manipulated. Seconds later, his nose seemed to heal on its own, expanding to its usual size, though blood continued to dribble from each nostril.

"What the hell are you doing here?" I demanded, drawing all my magic into my palms as subtly as I could. The smirk on Aden's lips suggested I was unsuccessful, but I was ready to fight fire with fire if I had to—and it was probably good that he knew it. "Do you have a death wish?"

"As I understand it, that's the usual assumption when people first meet me." He chuckled, and I noticed Darius's fist tighten. "I suppose I just ooze a natural charm."

I rolled my eyes and muttered, "That's one way to put it."

Aden's sneering sort of smile had the same enraging effect on

Darius that it had on me, and my dragon lurched forward, fist cocked as if to hit him again. The djinn sprung nimbly to the side, hands up.

"Ah, ah, ah, dragon," he sneered. "Would *you* finally like to experience the bite of my poison? It seems only fair, given how often your mate has—"

"Stop," I barked, then clambered out of the bed, the bed that I had wanted to spend the morning lazily making love in with Darius, and grabbed one of my dragon's shirts. I threw it on to cover my nudity, the shirt stopping about mid-thigh, and positioned myself between the two men. "Tell me what you want, Aden. I won't ask again."

Those black eyes darted between me and Darius, before finally settling on me as the djinn sighed. "Truce?"

"*What?*" I balked.

"I never wanted to hurt you, Kaye," he told me, and I felt Darius's temper start to boil again behind me. "Jasmine has my daughter captive. She's had her this whole time to ensure my compliance with her ridiculous demands. She... My sweet girl is a hybrid too, which is why I know so much about your kind. It's why I respect them as much as I do."

"Lies," Darius snarled, and I held up my arm to block him when he surged forward. "Djinns are known for their pretty words and tricks."

"We are," Aden agreed, darting back a few steps, his hands still up but no longer glowing with the thrum of his power. "I'll agree to that. I tricked you, Kaye. I did it over and over again, but I only did it to save my daughter. I would level whole cities for her," his hands pulsed blue suddenly, his eyes almost impossibly black, "but Jasmine has her tucked away. I won't risk her life."

"Kaye, you can't seriously—"

"The girl in the mirror's vision," I said suddenly, the image of the shadowy figure springing to mind. Blinking hard, I faced Darius. "Remember? We thought she might be tied up..."

"You saw her?" Aden asked—choked, more like. "Is she all right? Was she hurt?"

"It was hard to tell," I said, noting the way his hands trembled. "We saw her in the vision of a witch's black mirror. Our focus was Jasmine... But she looked tied up."

Aden turned away, his head bowed and his hands shimmering dark blue. He appeared to be attempting to control himself, his eyes clenched shut and his jaw tight. I glanced at Darius, who watched the djinn like a hawk. When his eyes met mine, I cocked my head to the side, wordlessly asking for his opinion. A slight shrug was his response, which was fair. Darius didn't know Aden.

Then again, neither did I.

But I *had* noticed, during our misadventures, that Aden responded emotionally when pressed about what Jasmine had taken from him. At the time, I had assumed it might be treasure or a valuable artifact of his own, and that his response was linked to his wounded pride. If this *was* true, that Jasmine had taken his daughter captive, then I was way off-base. Aden's desperation stemmed from a father's innate desire to keep his child safe. Plus, the idea that she was a hybrid certainly explained Aden's ardent fascination with them. The thought of there being someone else like me, someone tangible, unlike the figures in the wall art, made my stomach twist with excitement. I sighed softly. As interesting as the news was, *if true*, it still complicated things.

"Tell me everything," I ordered. "From the top. From the time Jasmine took her until now. The truth, Aden. It's the only way we'll help you."

"Kaye," Darius said sharply, and I met his stormy gaze.

"It's a child, Darius," I whispered. "We need to at least entertain the idea."

"Jasmine came to see me with one of her uncle's old lieutenants," Aden said softly, glaring at the hearth where our fire had once raged, strong and true against last night's summer storm. "She wanted my services—"

"As an assassin?"

He nodded. "But I didn't want the job. Capturing you... It sounded boring. So, she took my little girl while we were having our meeting... Jasmine's warlock brute threatened her. I had no choice but to concede."

"Djinns are powerful," I countered. "Couldn't you have just killed them?"

"It was too risky at the time. If there was crossfire and I accidentally..." He swallowed hard, then grimaced. "I'd never be able to forgive myself."

"So, you decided to kidnap me in exchange for your daughter's life," I stated, working through his reasoning in my head. "Was the artifact even necessary?"

"I may have told... a few white lies regarding the artifact," Aden said. He offered up a familiar impish grin when my gaze narrowed. As Darius began pacing behind me, perhaps needing to move so he didn't take another swing at Aden, I listened to the djinn's tale, searching for ways to poke holes in it—and coming up emptier than usual.

Apparently, Jasmine *did* want the artifact, but the purpose of the artifact was destruction, not protection. Aden and I were supposed to go through the hybrid-only trials, collect the artifact, then return to Jasmine, where she planned to drain my lifeblood to activate the artifact, and thus destroying all shifters.

"Hybrid blood is the one way to activate the artifact," Aden told me, leaning back against a boarded-up window with his arms crossed, "and Jasmine had a very *specific* shifter in mind to drain. However, she was furious when I returned without you. As far as she knows, that's why I'm here now... to kidnap you a second time before she loses her patience and kills Marie instead."

I looked at him sharply, noting the way his expression darkened. He'd slipped up and given her name. Marie. Names had power in the supernatural community, particularly amongst faes.

Lucky for him, I had no intention of using his own child against him.

"Warning your mate was part of her grand plan to draw all the shifter clans together again," Aden continued slowly. "Her goal is to use your blood to activate the artifact, then wipe out all those who gathered to oppose her in one fell swoop." He paused for a moment, his stare seeming to focus on something very far away. Then he cleared his throat and met my eye. "I *am* sorry for involving you in this. I was a fool to let my guard down in her presence."

"You'd do anything to protect your daughter," I muttered, ignoring Darius's incredulous scoff. "I get it."

"But I'll not let her win," Aden insisted, pushing off the wall and taking two steps toward me—before a sharp throat clearing from Darius made him stop. "I have a plan to stop her before she can even power the weapon."

"But you *gave* her the weapon. You went back to her and—"

"She believes I handed over the artifact, yes." Aden's grin turned twisted and cruel. "No one knows what the artifacts looks like... She swallowed the bait, along with my groveling and begging. It was quite the performance."

"Just like this is," Darius growled. He grabbed my arm. "Kaye, this is bullshit."

"Think what you want," Aden remarked with a dismissive shrug. "All that matters to me now is rescuing my daughter. That's all that has ever mattered. Your aim is to stop Jasmine... destroy her if you must. Our goals align."

"That's what you said last time," I grumbled, and the djinn sighed at me.

"I'd thought she would let Marie go in exchange for the arti-fact," he stated. "I thought she would send other goons after you, but I was mistaken. It won't happen again."

"A lot of people underestimate Jasmine's cruelty." I paused, giving the situation some thought. When my inner voice didn't express her concern, I had to go with my gut and trust Aden one last time. If he sullied that trust, I'd find a way to kill him once and for all. But if his daughter was in Jasmine's grasp, I could excuse *some* of the lying. "So, what's this plan of yours?"

"We'll return to her camp as though I've captured you—"

"Not happening," Darius snarled, his hands falling to my shoulder.

"*Together,*" the djinn continued, "we'll use your blood, just a bit of it, to activate the destructive power of the artifact and eliminate Jasmine once and for all. *I* will leave with Marie. *You* can return to this..." He glanced around, lips pursed. "...mountain paradise and avoid a potentially costly battle. A true win-win for everyone involved."

Except Jasmine, of course, but that was kind of the point. I glanced up at Darius, taking in the anger, the distrust, then looked back to Aden.

"Go on then," the djinn said. "Talk it over with your mate. Just know that this *will* work. I'll not leave my daughter with that foul creature one more day."

Which also suggested that even if I *didn't* go along with his clever little plan, Aden still might put it into action anyway. By force, if necessary.

"Darius, a girl's life is in danger."

Darius pulled me aside, scowling. "You know I won't let you go alone."

"Well, you'll probably want to stay to rally the troops anyway," Aden interjected. "Jasmine mobilized some of her army this morning, headed straight here. They're coming, but we could, in theory, annihilate them before they arrive. It all depends on you... and how long you want to stand around debating this."

Fuck me. All this information made my head spin, but it was glaringly obvious we didn't have time to wait. Swiping Darius's pants off the ground, I shoved them into his hands and told him to go warn the others.

"When you're done, we're going to finish this," I told him,

ignoring the way Aden did a little celebratory jig in my peripherals. "Together."

"Or not at all," he growled. He then dragged on his pants, glaring daggers at Aden as he went, and stalked out of the hall.

"Nice guy," the djinn said, grinning when I scowled back at him. "Seems like a real peach."

I exhaled, slowly closing my eyes, and pinched the bridge of my nose. "Just shut up, Aden..."

＃ 15 ＃

WHEN ADEN and I had traveled to Alfheim before, we took more traditional transportation methods. Walking. Driving. Portal hopping. Today, however, there was no time for any of that. Today, the situation was dire enough to warrant a bit of djinn teleportation.

"It'll feel just like going through a portal," Aden had insisted, planting a hand on both Darius's and my shoulders, then grinning. "Well, maybe a little harsher. Hope you had a light breakfast."

And then, before either of us could protest, he whisked us away from the Sanctius clan's mountains, where we left Quinn and Catriona behind, along with my father, to organize a counterattack against the troops Jasmine had supposedly sent marching our way at sunrise.

Teleporting with a djinn was *nothing* like moving through a portal. One moment we were standing there, minding our own business, and the next it felt like someone had tied a rope around our midsections and *yanked* with all their might. Footing gone. Bearings lost. The world blurred, but there were no rainbows to keep us company, no visions of the cosmos like we saw inside magic-powered portals. It was all a black and gray blur, until suddenly it wasn't. Until our feet landed hard, the impact shooting up our legs and hips and back, and suddenly we were somewhere else—fighting the urge to vomit everywhere.

I staggered away from the djinn, my hand over my mouth as I battled the nausea. Collapsing beside an unfriendly prickle bush, I dry-heaved as my eyes watered. Coughing, retching, I fought the desire to spew my very small eggs and bacon breakfast I'd had less than fifteen minutes earlier. An unsteady hand fell on my back, the palm hot, and although I knew Darius was just trying to comfort me, I waved him off, needing to come to terms with things on my own.

"'M fine," I muttered, wiping around my mouth. A quick glance up told me he wasn't faring much better: his face pale and clammy, his eyes teared, and he looked on the verge of fainting. Aden, meanwhile, appeared right as rain, dusting off his brown trench coat, cocking his head to one side as he appraised us. My eyes narrowed. "You couldn't have given us a bit of warning first?"

"Time is of the essence," he said snippily. "I think I gave you enough while you feasted—"

"A hardboiled egg and two slices of bacon from the camp is hardly what I'd call a feast," I fired back, my inner voice expressing her distaste for the djinn with a noisy gnashing of her teeth.

"Let it go, Kaye," Darius insisted softly. "We're here. We're alive. Just... Let it go."

"Okay, Mr. Black Pot." I accepted his hand when he offered it, my legs trembling under my body's weight once I was fully upright. He shot me a look, clearly not in the mood for snark, and I shrugged. "Sorry. You're right."

Hand-in-hand, we returned to Aden's side—only to survey what once appeared to be a thriving army's camp. Now? Not so much. Debris littered the open field. Smoldering mounds that must have once been bonfires continued to smoke, black spires rising up to a clear blue sky. A lone tent stood far in the distance, totally undisturbed—a tent whose walls matched those we'd seen in the black mirror.

"Have they all gone?" Darius demanded. "Every last one of them?"

"Well, yes, that's what I said earlier, but you—"

"Where are we?" I demanded. If the army had left, I had to assume they were within walking distance. "The landscape doesn't look all that much different from the range."

"That's because it isn't," Darius growled, stalking forward and taking in the sights—the young trees littered across the field, the flattened, yellow-green grass kissed by a faint summer drought, the gentle rolling hills beyond the tent. "We're near the mountains. I could have flown us here in under an hour."

"We didn't have an hour to spare," Aden hissed, grabbing Darius's arm when my dragon blitzed by him toward the field. Darius tried to wrench himself free, but this time the djinn had no issue in showing his full strength. I crossed my arms, biting the insides of my cheeks, as I watched him drag Darius back as one might pull a small child away from the store he *must* visit at the mall. Scowling, Aden thrust Darius toward me, and I managed to keep him from stumbling, then tightened my grip around his waist when he tried to lunge back for a second round with the djinn. Aden's scowl intensified. "We don't have time for *any* of this! Jasmine instructed me to meet her here, and I've ten minutes to go before my time is *up*. So, let's save this pissing contest until we've killed the bitch."

"You know I don't want to agree with him," I reasoned when Darius looked at me incredulously, "but I do. We're running on a time limit on every front here, Darius. Let's just... do what we came here to do."

As the pair glared at one another, I brushed my forearm over my chest as subtly as I could, ensuring that the second artifact, the copy-cat of the one in Aden's possession, was still securely in my bra. I'd been hiding it in different places since I returned to the Sanctius clan, and even though I wasn't sure it actually did anything, now seemed like the opportune time to find out.

"Jasmine will think that I've kidnapped Kaye," Aden stated when the snarling calmed down. His hands shimmered blue for a moment, producing a thick rope. "I need to make it look authentic."

"Absolutely not," Darius snapped before I could get a word in. "You can walk her in with a hand on her arm."

"Darius." I exhaled my frustration out. "I can do this. Ropes can't stop me from defending myself."

"Well, this might." When I glanced back, Aden had a knife in hand and a hapless look on his face. He shrugged when my eyes narrowed. "It needs to look real."

I could feel my dragon's temper flaring—hard—once again, but I managed to persuade him to take cover in the field. There were a few places he could situate himself in without being seen, though I knew the second I went with Aden, Darius would be following at a close distance. I couldn't fault him for that.

So, begrudgingly, Darius stalked off to hide himself. My inner voice expressed her palpable discontent at him leaving, but I ignored her. After we had... *bonded* last night, my inner voice was all about doing it again. As much as I would've rather been in bed with a naked Darius right now instead of allowing Aden to tie me up and hold a knife to my throat, there were more pressing priorities.

Being a mature adult sucked.

"Ouch," I hissed, flinching back when the tip of the knife poked a little too deeply into my skin for comfort.

"Sorry," the djinn muttered, holding it about an inch away from my throat as we stumbled across the field together. If Jasmine was watching at this point, I did my best to make it seem like I was struggling to free myself.

"Just... try not to make me bleed, okay?"

"It'll look better if you're a little roughed up."

"Not happening, Aden."

"It's just a suggestion."

I bit my cheek to keep from responding, priming myself to play the pissed off captive role as we drew nearer to the tent. An eastward wind cut across the field, forcing the door of the canvas tent open just enough to reveal a table inside. My heart skipped a beat. This was it. *This* was the tent we'd seen in the mirror. As we passed through the opening, Aden's grip tightened, and I sprang into action, thrashing about and demanding to be set free. He shoved me forward, and I collapsed in a heap on the floor, the scent of grass filling my nostrils as I gathered my bearings.

I froze at the sound of Jasmine's laugh.

"Kaye," she sneered, the tips of her boots coming into view as she strolled right up to me. "Always a pleasure."

At this point, I didn't need to *act* like I hated her, like I didn't want to be there.

"Go fuck yourself, Jasmine," I growled right back, then, for good measure, spat on her boots. She leapt back with a cry, as if my saliva ate right through the leather and burned her.

"You couldn't have put a muzzle on her?" she demanded. "You think I want to hear the mongrel speak?"

Fingers twined through my hair and wrenched me upright. I flinched back at the cold, biting metal of Aden's knife against my throat. His hands shook slightly.

"Look, you wanted her here, and I got her here. It doesn't matter if she's muzzled or not," he said, his voice unnervingly steady. It didn't take a genius to figure out why. Across the tent, behind Jasmine in the corner, sat a little girl in chains. Her eyes were red and dirty tracks ran down her cheeks, like she'd been crying and no one had bothered to clean her—for days. She had her father's black eyes and long, lustrous lashes, but her hair was a sandy reddish brown, perhaps courtesy of her mother.

He hadn't been lying about her. Marie, his little girl, was most certainly Jasmine's captive. My heart went out to her, to both of them. No one deserved to be in this situation, even if

Aden *was* an assassin-for-hire beforehand. Kids ought to be off-limits, but with psychos like Jasmine, that was rarely ever the case.

"She's here. Now, give me Marie, just as we agreed," Aden ordered in the silence that followed, and although I refused to look at her, I could feel Jasmine's cold, penetrating stare wandering over me. Did she think I was an imposter? I kept my gaze on Aden's daughter, hoping that if she met mine, she'd know she didn't need to be afraid anymore. We were here to get her out. The little girl, however, couldn't stop staring at her dad —and I didn't blame her. Fresh tears rolled down her cheeks, and even though I knew I was supposed to be struggling, to be foaming at the mouth and cursing Jasmine to the high heavens, all I really wanted to do in that moment was to wrap Marie in a big hug and apologize for whatever that psychopath had put her through.

But that wasn't my job.

The djinn who held me "hostage", the one who had lied and tricked and deceived—he was the only one who could make Marie's pain stop.

Jasmine studied Aden for a moment, her purple-painted lips pursed, then sighed. "Fine. Take your brat back. She's terribly boring, you know. All she does is cry for you. Worryingly codependent, djinn."

I winced as Aden's knife dug into me, but he quickly pulled back, as if catching himself letting too much emotion slip. Jasmine stalked toward a cowering Marie, and with a lazy flick of her hand the chains around the little girl disappeared. Just as Marie's chains vanished, the rope bindings around me fell slack too. Out of the corner of my eye, I caught Aden removing the true artifact from his pocket, his hand trembling again.

"Come here, sweetheart," he urged, and Marie all but flew across the tent, darting around me and crashing against her father. I seized the moment to stand, the ropes falling free, and savored the look on Jasmine's face when she turned back and found me free.

"What are you—"

"We have a parting gift for you," Aden growled as he positioned his daughter behind him, then extended his arm and showed off the artifact. Jasmine's thin brows furrowed, her confusion evident, and I couldn't help but smile.

"Aden gave you a fake artifact," I told her. "We thought it fitting to test its destructive power on someone who actually *deserves* to be destroyed."

Her hands curled to shaking fists, but before she could spit anything foul from that awful mouth of hers, I sliced my finger across Aden's blade, then pressed my bleeding tip to the center of the artifact. The onyx rock, once smooth and fine, blistered with power, as though my blood was filling unseen pockets. When I yanked my hand away, the artifact hummed with a soft white light—which gave me some pause. White tended to be a healing color, used for kinder magics and softer spells. Hardly a color of destruction...

Aden raised the artifact, and with a pulse of his natural power—the kind that sent me stumbling into the table—a surge of white light fired across the tent and slammed into Jasmine. The fae flew backward into the tent's canvas walls and brought the whole structure crashing down. Grabbing his daughter, Aden made a beeline for the exit, and I followed at his heels, pushing the plummeting thick tent material out of my way as we scrambled outside.

Darius was already jogging toward us, and I rushed forward to greet him, easily falling into his arms and hugging him tightly.

"Is it over?" he asked in my ear, his husky voice giving me chills. "Did you get her?"

"We got her," I whispered back. Over his shoulder, I spotted Aden clutching his daughter close, his hand on the back of her head and his eyes clenched shut. As much as I disliked the djinn for all that he had done to me, that moment between father and daughter *almost* made all his tricks worthwhile. Almost. He still had some serious apologizing to do.

Our moment of quiet victory was cut short when sharp, barking laughter erupted from inside the tent. We all whirled around to find a figure fighting her way out of the fallen canvas, and moments later Jasmine reemerged, unharmed.

"You *fools*," she spat, arms wide and hair askew—eyes crazy. "You cast the *wrong* artifact!"

Aden strode forward, bursts of magic cracking across the field from each djinn-blue hand. His spells hit true, nailing Jasmine directly in the chest, but she just kept laughing, totally unaffected. Frowning, I joined in, hurling whatever hexes and curses I could think of in the moment. They all landed—but none of them stuck. The echoes of our spellwork carried on over the field, sounding up into the hills. When they finally faded out, Jasmine cocked her head to one side, glaring at us, and then disappeared with a dainty little *pop*. Not only did she have fae speed on her side, but she must have mastered the art of teleportation. Aden and I looked to each other, my heart racing, and then spun back at the sound of another little *pop*.

Jasmine reappeared behind us, this time dragging a screaming Marie into her arms. She hoisted the girl up, an arm around her midsection, the other hand wrapped firmly around her thin neck.

"Your partner *deceived* you, djinn," Jasmine cackled, those cold blues darting between us. "The hybrid would have discovered *two* artifacts in the inner sanctum of the trials. There have always *been* two. One for destruction, and one for protection."

Unconsciously, my hand went to my chest, and I snapped it back down to my side, my cheeks flushed when I realized Jasmine had spotted the movement.

"I know you have it, mongrel," she sneered. "I only want *that* one. Give it to me, and I'll let your fellow abomination continue to draw breath."

"I will *kill* you, fae!" This time it was Darius who caught

Aden as the djinn rushed forth, knowing Jasmine wouldn't hesitate to harm Marie—even if the outcome wasn't death—just to prove a point. My dragon pushed the djinn back, a hand against his chest, throwing himself over the magical hand grenade before it wiped all of us out.

"You don't have to do this, Jasmine," I said, knowing she was beyond reason but also knowing that I had to at least *try*. "You're not Abramelin—"

"Tick-tock, mongrel," she fired back in a sing-song voice. "Her neck is like a twig... So pliant. So easily *snapped*."

"Marie!"

"Daddy!"

"Stop!" I shouted, raising my hands when the fae started to twist the little girl's head sharply to one side. "Stop. Here..."

I looked to Darius, then Aden, then back to my dragon. *What choice did I have?*

As if hearing my thought, Darius shook his head, his response clear. I had no other choice. Keep the artifact, kill Marie. Give Jasmine the artifact, risk the clan.

"We'll stop her, Kaye," Darius growled. "Just hand it over."

Destruction, Kaye. Destruction.

I swallowed hard. My inner voice didn't sound as though she approved, but I didn't care. I could never risk a child's life; Marie was innocent in all this.

So, I fished the second artifact out of my bra, then marched to Jasmine with stiff legs.

"Give me Marie."

"No." She grinned. "Artifact first, *then* you can have your half-breed back."

I hesitated, then thrust the artifact toward her when she started to twist Marie's head again, dragging a strangled whimper from the girl. Eyes alight with cruelty, Jasmine plucked the artifact from my hand—then disappeared with another little *pop*, taking Marie with her.

Aden's cry thundered across the landscape.

❧ 16 ❧

"Aden, I'm so sorry." I crouched before the fallen djinn, two seconds away from snapping my fingers in front of his deadened stare if it meant getting some sign of life out of him. After his anguished wail when Jasmine stole Marie for the second time, he had practically become comatose. While I didn't particularly enjoy his snark, the nothingness in his expression bothered me more. "Aden? We're going to get her back. We're not going to let Jasmine hurt her."

"I'm going to kill her," he croaked, and I sat back on my heels with a soft sigh.

"I know."

"It's our only option," Darius said, towering over the both of us. "She's beyond redemption."

"I'm not sure *how* we're going to do it when we endowed her with some insane hybrid-magical protection," I muttered. My hand fell to Aden's shoulder, giving him a small shake. "But we'll figure it out. This isn't the first time the odds have been stacked against us."

"You two go." He shrugged my hand off and stood, the navy-blue fog of his true self crawling up his neck, as though he couldn't be bothered to hide it anymore. His hands radiated with power, pulsing, surrounded by fog, and I shuffled out of the way, not wanting to get caught in a crossfire when he stalked by me. About ten steps away, he paused, barely looking back at us over his shoulder. "Go to your clan. Her armies will likely be there by now. They'll need you. *I will find Jasmine.*"

"Aden, we can do it together—"

"I will do it alone." He turned and tossed the protection artifact to me. "Protect your people. If you see Marie..."

"I won't let her out of my sight," I promised—and it was a promise I intended to keep. As Aden disappeared into thin air, leaving a rush of swirling blue-black smoke in his wake, I vowed that if I found Jasmine and Marie first, I wouldn't let either of them get away this time. I gripped the protection artifact tightly; first thing's first, however, was casting this thing over the Sanctius clan, the Brisbane dragons, and Zayne's militia. We had a tool to protect them now. I would never forgive myself if we were too late to actually use it.

"This is a clusterfuck," Darius said with a sigh. When I faced him, I noticed the way his lips twitched into a little half-smile. I raised an eyebrow, confused as to why he might be smiling at a time like this, and he shrugged. "We seem to do our best work knee-deep in clusterfuck territory. Why should today be any different?"

I swallowed hard and slipped the protection artifact in my pocket. "I hope you're right."

"It's been known to happen."

We stared at one another for a moment, the last moment of peace we'd have until all this was over, and ended it with the kind of kiss I'd remember when I was old and gray. The kind that stole my breath away, that made my toes curl—that roused my inner beast to life, hungry for more.

That kiss was all we had, and we both knew it. As we tore ourselves apart, I turned away to catch my breath, to steel my nerves. When I was ready, I took Darius's sloppily folded clothing and stepped back as he shifted. Something in me stirred at the sight of his dragon form, at the sunset-hue scales and the dangerous black spikes along his spine. Seeing him in dragon form was *always* impressive, always stirring, but this time it was different.

This time, the skittering feeling beneath my skin returned, the kind I had felt when I first watched my father and siblings take flight—the sensation of my innards *moving*. Adrenaline pounded through me, but it had to take a backburner. There was no time to revel in the sensation. No time to savor it, to explore it. We had to go.

The fate of hundreds of lives depended on us.

So, I climbed onto his back and prayed that we would live to see tomorrow morning.

JUST AS DARIUS HAD GUESSED, JASMINE'S CAMP HAD ONLY BEEN about an hour away from the Sanctius clan's mountain range. My best guess as to why our scouts hadn't noticed them before was that a powerful ward had been cast around the camp in its entirety, and once they left, Jasmine lowered it to allow Aden and I to enter and see the remains of what had been right under our noses the entire time. It seemed like something petty enough for Jasmine to do.

Unfortunately, just as Aden had guessed, by the time we returned, a battle was fully underway. We had spotted the blackness, tinged with bright pops of magical color, hovering over the range as we approached, and when we were near enough to take it all in, this battle was just as grisly as the last. Dragons swarmed the air, a few with riders on their backs, but there were hundreds and hundreds of gargoyles clogging up the skies, latching onto any of our allies with wings and tearing them apart. As Darius and I joined the fray, I blasted as many as I could, while my dragon melted dozens to a crisp with his ferocious alpha flame. Purple fire cut clear pathways across the airways, giving room for other smaller winged creatures to have a go at a few gargoyles themselves.

Witches on broomsticks buzzed around too, but unlike Abramelin's army, Jasmine's air force was primarily gargoyles. I imagined fewer sinister creatures were willing to join her horde after her uncle's defeat. Not only did Zayne have them on the run for the last few weeks, but Jasmine was *no* Abramelin. Still, gargoyles were a fearsome foe to combat, with their stone bodies blotting out the sun, their reanimated figures hell-bent on following their programming—courtesy of Jasmine's loathsome mind, no doubt.

Below, our ground troops clashed with Jasmine's armies of demons, dark elves, goblins, and other hellish beasts at the foot of the mountains. The fighting carried on up through the village. Halls smoldered. Open fires raged, gobbling up the dry grasses and underbrush of late summer. The sight of all those dark *things* invading the Sanctius clan—it stoked the fire burning in my belly, the fight within. Like an unwelcome visitor darkening my door, I hated the sight of all those foul creatures even being *remotely* near the Sanctius village.

The only creatures we could count on not being there were vampires, given that it wasn't even noon yet, but if the battle lasted into the night, there was no telling what other devils she had waiting in the wings. I hurled a hex and knocked out two gargoyles latched onto one of Darius's clawed feet, my mouth set in a thin line. There was no way in hell we were letting this last until the night.

We had to find a way to stop it before then. As I surveyed the battles below, I had to steel my heart to the sight. Bodies lay strewn about; too many had already died.

"We have to find Jasmine!" I shouted, blasting another

gargoyle who had a winged-fae in a headlock. The creature disintegrated as soon as my hex hit, and the fae shot us both a thumbs up before regrouping with another cluster of flying allies.

Darius's low growl suggested he agreed, and he veered sharply to the left, drawing away from the main site of aerial combat. The distance gave us a better vantage point, allowing us to see the battles above and below with more clarity. Although, in theory, Jasmine could be anywhere, I assumed she would come here. After all, she had the destruction artifact *and* a hybrid. It wouldn't take long to charge it and do serious damage to the people I held most dear.

In the distance, I caught a flash of familiar navy scales, and my enhanced sight honed in on Quinn in dragon form, his own powerful flame holding the gargoyles back as Catriona, seated on his back *without* a saddle, hurled curse after curse, hex after hex, at every enemy within sight. I blinked back my surprise, taking in her battle armor, her braided white-blonde hair. In that moment, she reminded me of a mythical Valkyrie—and I immediately decided it was an apt comparison.

My vision swam as I watched her, tears of pride, fear, and love trickling through. Sniffing, I wiped a thumb under each eye. Now was no time for tears.

Focus, Kaye.

"I am," I snapped, glaring up at my forehead before returning my enhanced sight to the battlefield. Now, Jasmine likely wouldn't be down with her troops. Last time she barely went near the actual fighting, steering clear of it in order to sucker-punch me. She would need somewhere relatively clear to fuel the artifact… I turned my attention to the peaks of the mountains, until I finally spotted her—*and* Marie, much to my immediate relief. "There!"

Darius swooped low without hesitation, dodging a few wayward blasts of magic as we sailed toward Jasmine and Marie. He angled his wings for braking, slowing our speed until we collided hard with the mountaintop, landing close to the alpha's hall—with its secret doorway into the belly of the range, where clan innocents lay hidden. It didn't surprise me one bit that Jasmine would try to make her last stand there, as if she could stroll right in and sit on Darius's alpha throne while her minions died for her below. Yeah. Not happening.

She sneered at us, though didn't seem surprised that we had tracked her down. Instead, she continued to shove Marie's bloody hand against the destruction artifact, fueling it with hybrid blood. We didn't have much time, and I sprang to action immediately. My first move: protect Marie. Reopening the cut on my finger, I pressed the bleeding digit against the protection artifact in my pocket, then slid off Darius's back as he roared at Jasmine. In the distance, our dragon allies roared back, the battle cry rousing the ground troops too, who responded with shouts of their own.

"Pathetic," Jasmine spat. Marie's pale body lay limply at her feet, her head bowed. There was no telling how long Jasmine had been bleeding her dry, but it stopped *now*.

Although I wasn't completely sure how to activate the artifact, I infused it with my white magic, noting the way the little pockets had already filled somewhat with my blood, then pointed it at Marie and fired. A burst of white light cracked across the distance between us, slamming into the poor girl and knocking Jasmine to the ground. Seizing the opportunity to get Marie out of there, I darted forward with a burst of fae speed, scooped her limp, little body off the ground, then raced back to Darius's side. I set Marie between his two front feet, noting that the protection of the artifact had sealed the gaping wound across her palm.

"You can't have her," I shouted at Jasmine as the fae staggered to her feet, her face twisted with rage. "She's protected now."

"I'd rather bleed *you* anyway, mongrel," she sneered back, her hair a mess—something that, in that moment, brought me more satisfaction than it should have. Beside me, I heard Darius's form shift from dragon to human, and I soon found him kneeling beside Marie, two fingers over her pulse, brow knitted. Across the way, I felt Jasmine drawing her power to her hands, both the artifact and her person primed for an attack. As my finger bled over the protection artifact, I mirrored her flow of magic, calling whatever white magic I had within the depths of my being to the forefront. Her lips twitched when our eyes met. "You think I'd kill the creature? Her blood makes the artifact *work*."

"There's a pulse," Darius said, almost begrudgingly, "but it's faint. Steady enough for now, but I'm worried we're losing her."

Foul... loathsome woman. Bleeding a child. My inner voice agreed, her disgust evident in the adrenaline pounding through my body, preparing me for confrontation.

"Kaye, use the protection on yourself," Darius urged. "You know she's gunning for you—"

I threw up a white magic shield as two blasts of magic hurtled toward us. The red and orange streaks of light hammered into my shield, the force behind them knocking me back a few paces. It was clear, however, that these curses weren't meant for me. They were aimed at Darius. Soon she would come after me, but not before butchering good shifters and supernaturals in the battle below. Her forces were deluded enough to follow her maniacal plan.

So, I didn't use the protection artifact for myself. I had fought Jasmine before. She might have learned a thing or two from her uncle, but she certainly didn't scare me. The people fighting below, the people dragged into this war because some bitch fae had a grudge against me and Darius—they were the ones who deserved the ancient hybrid's magic protection the most.

While still maintaining my conjured shield as best I could in front of Darius and Marie, I extended the artifact's protection down to our forces fighting below. I willed the surge of white light, moving like an unstoppable whitewater flood, rushing down through the village, envisioning its protection extending solely to the forces of *good*, then pushed it out to the skirmishes at the foot of the mountain. The magic took its toll on me—fast. So much power, so many people to save... Spots danced in front of my eyes, the kind that came just before a blackout, and I tried to blink them away. The artifact had limits, surely, and I noted the bulges shrinking around the onyx stone, needing more and more of my blood to fuel its power.

In my moment of weakness, I dropped the shield protecting Marie and Darius, but just as Jasmine geared up to take advantage of the situation, my dragon shifted.

His roar rattled the mountaintop, and as I continued to extend coverage to those who needed it most, Darius's enormous figure positioned himself directly between Jasmine and me. His wings flared, shielding Marie too, and his second roar sounded more like he was baiting our adversary, daring her to give it her best shot. My inner voice whimpered, a sentiment I shared. My dragon was strong, but Jasmine's magic was stronger.

"Darius!" My eyes widened as she pointed the destruction artifact squarely at Darius, and before I had the chance to summon more protection, he shot upward, the blast of wind from his huge wings knocking me back. I hit the ground hard, the protection artifact falling from my grasp. A strangled cry clawed its way up my throat when Jasmine fired, a surge of orange-yellow light emanating from her palm, gathering its strength, before blasting toward my dragon.

White and orange. A vision flashed across my mind's eye: it was just like the hybrid in that painting, standing between two battling armies, a white shield and an orange staff in hand. She wielded them both—but to what end?

The orange missed Darius, skimming over his shoulder as he darted out of the way, the beat of his powerful wings sending up dust and gravel from the mountaintop. Panicked at the sight of Jasmine charging up for another blast, I scrambled for the protection artifact. Darius bore down upon on our enemy, purple flames gathering in his snarled jaws. He was fast—but Jasmine was faster.

She fired off another blast of the destruction artifact.

And this time—she didn't miss.

❦　17　❦

DESTRUCTIVE MAGIC HURDLED from Jasmine's palm, heading straight for Darius, and the world slowed around me as I watched, helpless to stop it, unable to save him. Like the spear from the painting, it thrust up and sliced through Darius's left wing. He had tried to dodge. Wings flared up and back, he appeared to be trying to backpedal, to narrowly avoid that second blast, but it did him no good. The hit was true and fierce, and I clamped my hands down over my ears at his anguished cry as he veered hard to the right, slamming into the mountainside.

"*Darius!*"

Blocking out Jasmine's mocking laughter, I pressed my finger against the protection artifact, spilling more of my life's blood into the device, refueling it as fast as I could. My whole hand was a bloody mess at this point, my blood falling freely in long, dark streaks over my skin. When the bulges around the onyx stone swelled enough, I cast protection over my fallen dragon. Not far from me, I could see the enormous hole in his wing, the edges crisped and sizzled—as though fire had done the deed. White light enveloped him, protected him, and I felt my head spin just a little bit harder as I willed the artifact to keep him safe.

Beside me, Marie remained unconscious, but a quick glance

told me the artifact's protection was fading already. Maybe the spell hadn't been powerful enough when I cast it. Maybe I hadn't spilled enough blood. All I knew was that she was vulnerable, as was Darius—and, slowly, so was I.

But if the spell was fading from Marie, it had to be gone from Jasmine. I turned my narrowed gaze toward her, steeling myself against her giggles, against her cruel stare—against the powerful hum of magic in her palm.

"There are too many of them to protect, mongrel," she stated, her taunt followed by a rather witchy cackle. "How much are you willing to bleed to save them?"

Her sinister smile faltered suddenly, her eyes wide and *pissed*, and in my sideview a blue shimmering light flickered to life. Suddenly, Aden materialized out of nowhere, crouching over his daughter, his hand to her forehead, his expression surprisingly neutral.

"Her protection is fading," I told him. He continued to stare down at her, until his arm shot up, deftly deflecting a curse from the insane fae across from us. He cast it aside like it was nothing more than a fruit fly hovering around his face.

"Thank you," he murmured, scooping Marie's little body into his arms. He stopped Jasmine's next hex with no more than a look, the blast of violet light stopping dead in its tracks, frozen midair, before it shot back at its caster. Jasmine shrieked and leapt out of the way, covering her head as a boulder behind her exploded into a thousand little pieces once the hex hit. The djinn's black eyes slid over to me, taking me in slowly. "I'll not forget this."

A chill raced down my spine at the eerie calmness in his tone.

To me, Aden had never been more frightening than in that moment. Utter serenity. Calmness. Not a tremor in sight, either in his voice or his hands.

I knew that if he could have it his way, he would have ripped Jasmine to pieces with his bare hands.

"Wait." He had already started to disappear, spires of black and blue fog rising around him. I caught the sob before it left my throat, swallowing it with some difficulty. "Take Darius. She hit him with the artifact... Take him somewhere safe."

We both looked in my dragon's direction, and I found him in human form. His left arm was a bloody, mangled mess—the forearm and wrist twisted a completely different direction from his bicep and shoulder, his skin shredded. He appeared to be trying to get up, to find his footing, and to watch him struggle—it broke me.

"Please," I pleaded. Jasmine was also clambering to her feet, and it wouldn't take much from her to knock him down again. "Aden, I'm begging you..."

The djinn disappeared in a cloud of dark smoke, a smoke that shot over to Jasmine, knocked her over again—hard, from the grunt she made—then sped to Darius. My dragon tried to swat it away with his good arm, shouting for me, but the smoke quickly consumed him.

Then disappeared. Darius. Aden. Marie. All gone. I pressed my wounded finger harder against the protection stone, moving shakily to my feet. There was no one left on the mountaintop but Jasmine and me—and that was just the way I wanted it.

The irritated fae pushed herself up, dusting the flecks of mountain from her hands, then wrestled herself out of her too-tight leather trench coat. Beneath, she wore a black tank-top and black leather pants. Her boots appeared military-grade, perhaps lined with lead for stomping on her enemies. But in that moment, she looked small. Abramelin had oozed power. When I saw him on the battlefield, battling multiple enemies with ease, I had known he was the kingpin behind everything. *He* was the puppet master, a god among men—all that crap. Jasmine was just... ordinary. Deranged, sure, but she wasn't a god.

Nowhere close.

Destruction artifact clutched in her tight fist, she paced back and forth for a moment, looking very much like a caged animal —some uncontrollable wild thing. I had to give her that. She paled in comparison to Abramelin as the leader of this rebellion against the established order, but she radiated primal, raw energy.

"Fucking… djinns," she snapped, her hands trembling as she stalked to the edge of the mountain. With her back to me, I thought her foolish, but as my essence poured out into the protection artifact, I realized she was right to leave me to myself. In my effort to save the others, I was doing her job for her. I loosened my grasp on the artifact, hoping it was almost charged, and then willed a sliver of white magic to close the wound—but not heal it. I suspected I'd need it again soon.

I drew a soft breath, deciding to take *one* short moment to offer her an out. "Jasmine, you—"

"You might have protected your people," she said, her voice carrying on the wind, "but mine outnumber yours. In time, their protection from the artifact will fade, and I will cut them down… one by one."

"You don't have to," I argued, but my words lacked conviction. Jasmine had made up her mind. A part of me wondered if I was only saying this, going through the motions, so I'd have no regrets when this was all over. Jasmine whipped around, her expression suggesting I'd insulted her. I shook my head. "That isn't the way this all has to end. We can stop it. We can bring peace to the supernatural world once and for all. You are not your uncle."

"No," she sneered, her ice blue eyes narrowing, "I am not. *I* know not to underestimate you. *I* will not be butchered by my own *weapon*. They all worship his memory, but I would never be so *stupid*."

Right. So much for extending the olive branch. I exhaled softly and placed the protection artifact in my pocket, zipping it closed to ensure I wouldn't lose the precious stone.

"I saw your worthless half-brother down there," she admitted, stalking toward me like a predatory cat. "When I'm finished with you, I'm going to show him your broken body, whatever's left of it, so that will be his last memory before he dies."

I knew she wanted me to think about Zayne—and, by extension, everyone who mattered to me out there on the battlefield. My father was somewhere in the skies, fending off gargoyles and dodging witch hexes. Leda and Hudson, the siblings I'd only *just* started to connect with, would be alongside him, fighting a war they wouldn't have even been involved in if it wasn't for me. Catriona. Quinn. Darius's youngest brother, Hayden. *All* of them. Jasmine wanted to use my love, my friends, against me.

But not today.

I squared my shoulders, holding her cold stare as my hands hummed with magic. I could practically hear my inner voice smirking, if she had a face, a low rumble emanating from the depths of my soul. My very own battle cry. My very own dragon's roar.

"Are you ready, mongrel?" Jasmine demanded, bursts of neon light surging from her palms and wrapping up her arms. She cocked her head to the side, waiting, and I rolled my eyes.

"Fuck you, Jasmine." I called on whatever power I had left in me, ignoring how utterly drained I already felt from giving my life's blood to protect the others. I could bounce back. I could do this. I could beat her. "This ends today."

"With *you*," she growled before hurling all the energy she had building in her hands at me. Rather than forming a magical shield, I just ducked and rolled, feeling the heat of the magic, feeling the *hate* of it, grazing across my back. While the warmth made my heartbeat quicken, the magic didn't hold. Instead, it slammed into the stone walkways between Darius's home and his alpha hall, throwing chunks of gray and black up and leaving an enormous crater in its place. Jasmine fired again and again, and I found myself leaping, rolling, dodging, and calling on my fae speed to avoid the blows. While tiring, I knew I'd drain myself more producing a shield. With how I was feeling, conservation was key.

At the sound of her shriek of frustration, I seized the moment and fired off several curses whose only purpose was to cut, slice, and maim. Although I usually preferred to simply render an opponent unconscious, Jasmine would find a way to keep sticking her fucking bigoted nose in my life, one way or another, whether she was imprisoned or not.

The only way to stop Jasmine was to permanently silence her hate.

It didn't sit well with me, but when I thought back on all the vile things she had said about my loved ones, about how she had captured and *drained* a child, I knew I'd be able to deliver the final blow when the time came.

While she deflected most of my magic, one sliver of a slicing curse managed to slip through her defenses and leave a nasty cut along her cheekbone. She lifted a quivering hand to it, her eyes narrowing at the smear of blood on her fingers before zeroing in squarely on me.

"We don't have to do this, Jasmine," I told her. "We can end this without killing each other."

"You took my uncle," she spat, and I barely managed to avoid the trio of bright pink hexes she sent me way, rapid-fire and scarily accurate. The third clipped my shoulder—like a rogue bullet, the magic seemed to pass right through me, and I gasped through the searing pain. Jasmine remained uncharacteristically quiet after the hit; I would have expected her to gloat. Instead, she just stared at me, her cheeks flushed. "You *killed* him like he was a *human*. No magic. No sorcery. Just a knife. You gutted him and left him to die."

"He was strangling me," I choked out, and we engaged in a familiar dance for a few moments: spells and curses zinging back and forth between us, most missing, some colliding in the middle and exploding in a firework display of color and crackling power. When we both ceased fire, seemingly at the same time, I tried to catch my breath. "If I hadn't done something, I'd be dead. You can't blame me for that."

"Of course, I can," she spat, her voice cracking, "because then *he'd* still be alive—"

"And thousands of innocent people would be slaughtered!"

"Shifters aren't people," Jasmine stated, a sick sense of finality in her tone. "Neither are hybrids. The world would be a better place without them. I'm not sure where that traitorous djinn took Darius, but when I'm finished with you and your mongrel-sympathizing half-brother, I'm going to skin that dog alive for all his clan to see. A fitting ending to an *enormous* waste of space, I think."

"You," I growled, my whole body quivering—the skittering feeling of movement under my skin returning as a rush of heat washed over me, "are never going to touch him *again.*"

A vision of Darius in that blood-soaked field, crawling for safety yet dying alone, flashed across my mind. This time, Jasmine's cruel laughter surrounded it, pervaded it, and my knees buckled. I fell forward with a cry, my hands slamming down against the mountain.

"What the hell are you doing?" Jasmine snapped. "I haven't done anything yet. Or is that mongrel brain of yours finally turning on itself?"

Something in my brain was clicking into place, something slow and dusty, new and unused. I blinked hard, trying to fight my momentarily shrouded vision, as adrenaline pounded through my body. My palms turned clammy. My heart hammered against its confinement, and for a few seconds there, I felt like I was about to die. Rushing, pulse-pounding anxiety ripped through me, akin to that of the worst panic attack I'd ever experienced— compounded. I cried out again at the sight of something slithering beneath my skin, creeping up my arms, until my elbows bent forward of their own accord, snapping into place. A dull pain radiated up and into my shoulders, and when I tried to cry out again—a guttural, familiar *growl* slipped out instead.

"Kaye..." Jasmine's voice sounded rather far away, so distant and outside of my own existence that I barely noticed it anymore. Instead, my body seized the moment, my bones bending and snapping, my skin turning ashen—then a brilliant green. My field of view went from staring at the ground to Jasmine's knees, then up some twenty feet in the air, towering over her. The pain rocking my innards disappeared, and for a moment I felt as though I'd just been put through the ringer by a massage therapist. Everything felt stretched yet taut, almost pleasantly sore. I blinked, but I saw no fluttering red eyelashes. Black lashes swept down and over my eyes with each blink.

The adrenaline faded. My heartbeat sounded slow and steady —and *firm*, if possible.

I had shifted.

All that pain, all that anxiety—it was the pain of rebirth. There was no more inner voice, for she was me and I was her. We looked through the same eyes, moved through the same body. Jasmine stood there, smaller than before, and stared up at me with an expression that suggested she was about to vomit. I huffed, filling my enormous new lungs and exhaling sharply, and noted that smoke rushed from my nostrils.

If only I had a mirror.

From what I could see, I was green and enormous. My scales were somewhere between emerald and pine green, and my toenails—claws—were solid black, onyx like the artifacts. I wasn't sure what to move to make things work, but I extended and flapped my wings without *trying*, my new body responding on instinct alone. Taking a few seconds longer for myself, I looked back over my form, which extended a long way behind me. Like Darius, black spikes lined my spine, though I had a smattering of smaller spikes surrounding the large ones too. My tail reminded me of a porcupine. God help whoever was on the receiving end of *that*.

Speaking of which...

I crouched low, returning my unflinching stare to Jasmine. I saw the world more clearly now, even without my enhanced fae senses. It was like someone had put new lenses in front of me and sharpened the clarity to an insane degree. I saw edges, ridges and hems, no matter the distance, clear as day.

And what I saw, clearest of all, was the fear in Jasmine's eyes as she glared up at me. I snarled, noting the way she flinched back, and lowered my head to so that I could look her dead in the eye. Then, heat crawled up my throat, bubbling up from my gut—almost like a burp, embarrassingly enough—and when I tasted the flames on the edge of my tongue, I opened my snarling mouth to accommodate.

A sea of black flame surged toward her. Black and beautiful and *hot*.

Jasmine screeched and leapt out of the way, but only just. When the flames died in my throat, I noted the scorched path along the mountaintop stone, headed straight for her and stopping a mere foot from her current position. Knowing Jasmine, however, she wouldn't be down for long, and I wasn't sure if I had access to my magical abilities in this form. Not wanting to risk it, I charged. Even without magic, I had brute strength and an enormous weight on my side, not to mention four feet laden with sharp, black claws and a spiked tail.

The fae attempted to get herself upright *and* fire off another round of destructive magical power my way, but she wasn't successful at either.

Trying to do too many things at once, I thought, chuckling in my head. Too bad I couldn't verbalize any of my zingers. Still, my sneering sort of roar-bark seemed to do the trick. Jasmine's cheeks darkened as she scrambled, boots slipping on the stone underfoot, and even her use of fae speed wasn't enough to help her. Each of my steps was four of hers, and I effortlessly caught up with her—and trampled her into the ground before she could teleport. Each foot stomped over her, and I leapt to the side to see if my handiwork had finally done the deed.

Gasping, Jasmine continued to flee, only this time she was crawling, one of her legs limp and twisted from the knee down. She had to realize by now that these were her last precious moments to convince me to spare her, to tell me that she was willing to change, that she could temper her hate and learn to live in a community that encompassed all different kinds of creatures, not just the ones she deigned acceptable.

"Trust a *dog* to not l-look where she's walking," she sneered, and I let out a deep, long breath, smoke rushing down at her, my disappointment palpable—but not entirely unexpected. Blood dribbled down her nose, and I realized she was favoring her right hand, using it to drag her body down and away from the mountain peak toward the rest of the village. I followed, slowly, cautiously, assuming she wouldn't just surrender without a fight.

She made it to the somewhat steep hill leading down to the upper-most clan halls. While I had seen fighting on the way up, it seemed the bulk of the battles had moved into two distinct arenas: land and sky. The circling dragons had taken care of most of the gargoyles, but the witches appeared to be giving them a run for their money. Below, the lines between armies were murky, difficult to tell who was who. Dragon vision was clearer, sharper, than an average person's, but I couldn't zoom in as much as I could have as a fae.

"I think you broke my back," Jasmine spat, coughing up blood and letting it drip onto the ground. Slowly, she lifted her head, her teeth stained red, and laughed. "But it d-doesn't matter, mongrel. It doesn't matter if you kill me. *My* people will annihilate your people before the day is done. All those f-fools, above and below, are going to die... and it's all your f-fault."

I stomped my front feet, growling, fire burning its way up my throat in protest, then willed myself to settle at her laughter. This was what she wanted. She wanted me to *feel*.

Or, as I soon realized, she wanted me distracted.

Bringing her wrist to her mouth, I watched in horror as Jasmine ripped into her tender, pale flesh with her teeth. Blood gushed in dark red spurts, as though she had severed a vein, and before I could stop her, she slammed the destruction artifact against the wound, as if forgetting *her* precious "pure" blood wasn't the kind the artifact needed, flopped down on her side—and unleashed holy hell with her uninjured hand. A pulse of orange-yellow magic shot out from her palm, more powerful and more potent than anything I'd seen thus far. The last of the destruction artifact. All that it had left. Like an enormous strobe light, the kind search-and-rescuers used to cut through a raging storm, the destructive magic sliced through anything in its path: halls, schoolhouses, trees, rocks. It then ripped across the battle-field, butchering all it touched.

My cry of despair sounded throughout the valley. Trust Jasmine to drag down as many as she could on her deathbed. A fitting end—one that I decided to hasten. Summoning my fire once more, I showered her with black flame. Within seconds the destructive beam of light disappeared, but the screams from below filled my ears no matter how hard I forced the fire out. Her laughter died along with her, an intermingling of cries and cackles, short-lived, that would haunt my dreams.

Dead, Kaye. My inner voice didn't say it, but I somehow understood it to be true. Unable to sustain this form, this fire, for much longer, I stopped my flame and shifted back to my half-fae form. The shift *back* was less painful than the initial turning. Much faster, too. It felt similar to that moment when hovering between sleep and awake, then suddenly jolting upright because it felt like a fall into the abyss. My line of sight fell as my dragon body shrank into my fae body—and I wasn't sure where it all went.

Unable to hold myself up, I let my knees collapse, blinking hard in an effort to adjust from the sharpened sight to my usual, everyday sort. Naked, bleeding, gasping for air, I raised my head and found myself staring at blackened earth—and ash. Just as Darius had roasted her uncle to death, I'd turned my enemy to dust, a little bit of nothingness that caught in the breeze and scattered toward me. I closed my eyes, bracing against it, then threw myself forward and vomited everything that was left in my stomach onto the mountain.

Shaking, I crawled forward, gritting my teeth as rock cut into my knees and palms I searched around the scalded ground for the destruction artifact. Moments later, I found it—totally unharmed. Eager for more blood. Ready to unleash *more* chaos. I shook my head and let it fall. No more destruction. I pushed up on unsteady knees, tears spilling down my face as I gazed at the valley of death and blood below.

No more.

I wobbled back to my shredded clothes and searched through them until I found the protection artifact. Dirt and blood and soot smeared across my body as I shuffled back to the edge of the mountain, one step at a time, the pain of my be-all-end-all battle with Jasmine trickling across my system. I gasped sharply, the wound in my shoulder stinging as I curled my arm to hold the protection artifact to my chest. I could heal the gash— but then I wouldn't have the white magic to power the artifact.

And in that moment, I chose them over myself. I chose the people fighting and dying for our cause. I chose the hundreds of supernaturals and shifters who had been dragged into this horrific fight for no other reason than a fae supremacist wanting revenge—to fill her uncle's grotesque shoes.

Tears fell harder when I reached the edge, my chest rising and falling in uneven bursts as I realized Darius was nowhere to be seen.

My lips quivered. I hadn't told him I loved him one last time before Aden took him.

He'd known, of course. Hopefully.

I reopened my wound on the sharp edge of a stone, then sliced a new one across my palm and gripped the artifact tightly. My dragon would know I did this for him, for the others, for the survival of our cause—but he needed to know just how desperately I loved him.

I raised my hands, one clutching the artifact, the other palm forward, shaking. My head spun and my stomach roiled. My bones wanted to crumble in on themselves and my mind yearned for sleep's sweet embrace.

And it would have it. Soon, probably. My lips parted, and I whispered my last words, hoping the wind might carry them to the man I loved.

"This is for you," I whispered. "I love you."

Seconds later, a brilliant white light swept through the village and swarmed the valley. I squeezed the artifact harder, fueling it with more of my blood. The light intensified. Protection wrapped around my militia, my family, and my fae sister on the back of her dragon.

Kaye...

"I know," I murmured, closing my eyes tightly, tears streaming down my cheeks, "and it's my choice."

❧ 18 ❧

"KAYE!"

We already talked about this, I thought to myself sleepily, my eyes opening and closing in slow, uneven beats. *This is my choice.*

"Kaye!"

I want to do this for them.

"Oh my god..." Footsteps crashed across the rocky mountain peak, falling like muffled thunder as I drifted in and out of this world. "*Kaye!*"

"My choice," I whispered. My brow furrowed when I realized that the voice desperately shouting for me didn't belong to my inner voice. The logical side of me pushed through the brain fog: the voice all but screaming my name was a man.

Large hands slammed onto my shoulders, catching me before I pitched forward. I blinked slowly, unable to focus, then looked down when a warm, *clean* T-shirt was wrapped around me. So warm. I closed my eyes. Like someone had just taken it out of the dryer.

"Kaye?" The voice cracked, and slowly I was eased backward, my body crumbling against a hard chest. "Kaye, say something."

I watched familiar hands skim my body, hovering over the

broken bits, the bruised skin, the blood. Thick fingers. Muscular forearms. Skin dotted with dark little hairs...

"Darius?" I croaked, not believing it for a second. Aden had taken him away. Jasmine had nearly killed him. He... Maybe this was heaven. Maybe there was an afterlife.

"It's me, sweetheart," I heard him rumble in my ears. "Kaye, give me the artifact."

Cradled in his arms, my gaze followed those magnificent hands as they went for the bloated onyx stone, slick and full of blood. When I realized he was trying to pry it from my grasp, I shook my head weakly and held more tightly.

"If I do, they'll die." Even now, as my weakened body started to succumb to the blood loss, my reasoning behind all this was clear. "Now, they can live."

"But you'll die," Darius argued. He leaned down, using both hands now to wrestle the stone from me. Slowly, I turned my head to admire his handsome profile. This had to be heaven. He looked so... clean. Untouched by this gruesome battle. I lifted my other hand, the white light of protection no longer flowing from it—but if the artifact kept getting my blood, the spell cast would remain. Gently, I trailed my fingers over his chin, nails catching on the scruff.

I hummed happily, letting my hand fall—too weak to keep it up. "Darius... I'll die for them. Don't be sad."

"Kaye—"

"They deserve to live," I argued, holding the stone even tighter. It bit into my hand despite its smoothness, the pain sharp and precise.

"*You* deserve to live," he growled. "*Give me the artifact.*"

"I have to save them."

"Kaye."

"They'll die. I-I can't let them die because I... I..."

"Kaye, listen to me." He hoisted me up suddenly, the jerky motions making me dizzy, and carried me away from the edge. After setting me down against a rock, he crouched in front of me. Behind him, I noticed, figures stood cloaked in shadows—blurred. My dragon grasped my chin, forcing me to look at him. "Kaye, if you die, *I'll* die. Do you hear me? I will *die* without you. I might live until I'm a hundred, but every day without you will be like dying a slow, agonizing death."

"N-No." Tears rolled down my cheeks. Why was he saying this? He could go on and *live* a full life as the Sanctius alpha, with or without me. The thought of him suffering, dying, each day... I shook my head, lip wobbling. "*No.*"

"You are my mate," he insisted firmly. "You are my life. Without you, I don't have a life. Sacrificing yourself for the good of others..." He shook his head, smiling slightly. "Kaye, that's one of the thousand reasons why I love you. You'll be the perfect alpha's wife, mother to the clan, because of it. But, sweetheart, you can't go right now. I need you. *We* need you." His hand wrapped around my bloody fist. "Please, give me the artifact."

My dragon—so persuasive. I didn't have to think about it; his words struck a chord. Slowly, one by one my fingers loosened around the protection artifact, until finally Darius was able to wriggle in and yank it from my hand. Blood dropped onto the rock at my back in fat, slow droplets, and I vaguely heard Darius demanding medical attention—immediately. I studied his face, my lips curled into a dreamy smile. He was *so* handsome. I reached for him, but found I couldn't lift my arm at all this time.

"*Now,*" Darius shouted, and suddenly the shadowy figures behind us lurched forward. No longer shadows, they came into sharper focus the nearer they came, the most familiar of them—Catriona. My smile tried to grow as she fell to her knees beside me and shoved Darius out of the way.

"Oh my god, *Kaye,*" she cried, tears streaming down her cheeks. Why was she crying? Where was *her* dragon? I blinked up at her, finding I lacked the energy to speak. She was so beautiful, my warrior, goddess best friend. She wrapped her hands around my bleeding palm as a few others crowded in around me, their faces only distantly familiar. All faes. Hands pressed to various parts of my body, the initial contact sharply painful. Cupping my ribs. Curling around my knee. Pressing against my shoulder. Biting agony made me wince, but within seconds all I felt was warmth.

Catriona's white magic glowed brightly around my hand, her blue eyes locked on mine.

"Don't you ever do that to me again," she said, half-laughing, half-sobbing. "You're going to be fine. Just try not to move."

"Hi, Catriona," I whispered, my mouth moving like it was stuffed full of cotton balls. She smiled, her eyes shimmering.

"Hi, Kaye."

"You look like a Valkyrie," I told her, though she probably only heard *you* and *Valkyrie*, my voice's strength fading in and out. Catriona nodded at me all the same.

"Just relax," she told me kindly. "You'll start to feel better soon..."

I let my head fall back against the rock, wondering what she could possibly mean by that. I already felt *great*. Everything was so warm and soft. No more pain. Slowly, however, as I watched dark shapes flit across the sky, occasionally pursued by something much larger and making an awful lot of noise, the world came back into focus. I could hear the chatter of soft conversations around me, see the faces of faes healing me. Some of their names even came to mind. Slowly, the fog started to lift, and memories of what had only just happened came flooding back.

"Darius?" I said, sitting up sharply and hissing at the jolt of pain blooming from my shoulder. Catriona told me to sit back—ordered was more like it—and moments later my dragon was by my side. I stared up at him, eyebrows raised, and let out a laugh that sounded half-mad. So, I hadn't just concocted him in my last sane moments. Smiling, I fluttered my eyelashes up at him. With so many healers working on me, my lashes were about all I could move, but I leaned into his hand when he placed it against my cheek. "You're *real*."

"I am," he said, chuckling. "I'm real and I'm here."

"How?" Before he materialized out of nowhere beside me, I remembered that Jasmine had struck him with the artifact. Then Aden. Then nothing.

"Your djinn fixed me right up after he tended to his daughter," my dragon explained, his thumb stroking my dirty, bloodied cheek. "He put me in some clothes, got my arm sorted out, then sent me back to win the war, I guess."

"Did he come with you?" It didn't surprise me when Darius shook his head, though he did it without a hint of malice or distaste. Clearly Aden had stayed behind with his daughter. No one could fault him for that. "And the battle? I tried to... Jasmine, she used the artifact... I..."

"You saved a lot of people, Kaye," he told me. Suddenly, an explosion erupted from somewhere below. Nowhere near enough to see the damage, but it shook the mountain. My healing committee huddled in around me, and when they finally moved away, muttering to each other, I noticed huge black plumes of smoke rising toward a clear, blue sky. There was no telling who the explosion hurt, us or them.

"I saw you shift," Catriona interjected, her white magic doing wonders for my shoulder wound now. "You were magnificent. And Darius is right... You protected pretty much everyone who survived Jasmine's attack."

"The numbers are on our side," Darius assured me as I looked between them, his face aglow with a sense of pride I'd never seen before. I had seen him proud of me before, of course, but this was something else. Something softer. Something more personal. My concern for the others, however must have been palpable, because Darius and Catriona continued to coddle me, telling me that the tide had turned and we were *winning*, and reminded me to just relax.

At that point, as strength began to seep through my body once more, I couldn't be sure if they were telling the truth or just trying to keep me complacent as the healers worked their magic. I appreciated it either way.

And I showed my appreciation by shooting upright, finally able to push everyone aside, and blasting an encroaching demon —crab-walking toward us with its deformed limbs and stretched, ash-white skin. The blast of green magic sliced right through the creature, splitting it in two. A few of my fae healers obliterated the two halves as they continued to skitter towards us, and I sat back with a weary sigh, the exertion taking more out of me than I cared to admit.

"Are you done being a hero now?" Catriona asked, her tone suggesting she was both teasing *and* lecturing. The hand on her hip suggested as much too. "Can I just heal you now, for goodness sake?"

"Have at it," I said, my cheeks reddening as Darius smirked down at me. "I think I've given all of me that I can today..."

Tomorrow, when I was well and recovered, I'd start to give again. By Darius's side, I'd help rebuild. I'd help rehome. I'd help recover all that we had lost today.

And for the first time since all this started, since Aden dragged me away from the man I loved, I felt confident in assuming there would even *be* a tomorrow.

＊ 19 ＊

"All right, out with it," I ordered, nudging Catriona with my shoulder and grinning. "Are you going to tell me how you managed to ride on Quinn's back without burning yourself or *what?*"

My best friend blushed, her gaze fixed on Darius's younger brother as he tried to weave his way through the celebratory crowd in front of us. Every time he seemed to find a way through, dancing, inebriated members of either the supernatural militia or Sanctius clan cut him off, making Catriona and I giggle like teenagers from our spot at the table.

All around us, celebrations from yesterday's victory reigned. While I had initially feared the battle with Jasmine's forces might drag well into the night, we managed to put an end to things in a tight two hours—a record for a skirmish of that size. When Jasmine's forces realized their fearless leader had once again been burned to a crisp by one of the Sanctius dragons, most broke ranks and fled. The ones who had stayed were dealt with by ground forces and war-ready dragons alike, until eventually our side had rid the mountain range and the lands around it of Jasmine's evil stain.

That night had been for healing, for gathering the dead, and for sending wounded fighters home. Darius and I, after the healers had set me right, worked tirelessly into the wee hours of the morning to ensure everything went off without a hitch, which included hiding the hybrid artifacts deep within the Sanctius mountains—separately, so that only we knew their locations. Brisbane dragons, my father at the helm, escorted supernaturals back to portals, and after a quick nap in the alpha's hall, they had left this morning for home—just before the party started. After everything that had happened, no one wanted to sit in sorrow for long, and the whole village—whatever was left of it— succumbed to feasting, dancing, drinking, and an all-out victory party since breakfast. Rebuilding could begin tomorrow.

I'd had, oh, about three hours sleep since yesterday, but there was no way I'd miss the celebrations. Not after Catriona and the other faes had saved me, and we had *finally* won the war. Not just a battle. The war. Period. Zayne had started organizing search parties to bring in higher-ranking members of Jasmine's armies for trials in Alfheim, and while a few of his captains had already started the task, I'd assured him he could, in fact, take a day off to party with the rest of us.

The last time I'd seen my fae half-brother, he'd been face-deep in a wood nymph's cleavage. Frankly, considering where that probably took him, I didn't *want* to see him anytime soon. After all, I had enough of my loved ones here in the alpha's hall. Catriona. Darius—the man of the hour. As the healers worked on me, he had left my side—after I all but twisted his arm—and led the final charge in battle, effectively securing our victory. It didn't surprise me that we'd barely said two words to each other since the celebrating started, but I had more than enough people to keep me busy. My new family. My best friend. Darius's siblings and his mother.

I'd never been happier, honestly.

"Kaye," Catriona said softly when Quinn was swept up again by the dancers, "I learned something interesting recently regarding... *that* subject."

My eyebrows shot up, hands around my ice-cold drink. "Oh, really?"

"It was in one of the old history books in the library off the alpha's receiving hall," she explained, her cheeks darkening with every word. "While dragon shifters won't burn each other, no matter what form they're in when they touch, supernaturals can *only* touch them if they are their true mate. Darius gave me blisters when I touched his scales because he and I were never meant to be, but Quinn and I... Well, I could ride him in the battle because, he and I... We..."

I pressed my lips together, trying not to giggle at my bestie's floundering. Apparently, I wasn't the only fae that fate and destiny, those crafty bitches, had paired with a Thomas shifter. Unable to watch her fumble around for the right words, I threw my arms around her and hugged her tightly.

"We're *really* going to be sisters now, aren't we?" I whispered in her ear, then squealed happily when her head bobbed up and down. Catriona had always been my sister in spirit. A fae sister by blood. But now, if we did as fate and destiny commanded, we'd be truly family for life.

When we pulled apart, Quinn had finally hacked his way through the dance floor, arms up and drinks coasting over people's heads as he squirmed free.

"What is it about my face," he demanded as he stalked back to our table, one of dozens scattered around the alpha's hall, "that suggests that I want to *dance?* Am I giving off some sort of *vibe* that I'm unaware of?"

Catriona and I laughed as he handed a drink to my best friend, his expression decidedly grumpy. It lightened, however, the second Catriona stood and grabbed his arm, downing half her drink in the process.

"Does that mean you won't dance with me?" she asked, fluttering her lashes up at him.

The dragon shifter grinned, then set his drink down at our

table and scratched at the back of his neck. His cheeks darkened. "I... Well, I'll always dance with you."

I made a cracked whip sound, flicking my hand for emphasis, and his eyes narrowed at me before Catriona dragged him away in a fit of giggles. As I watched the noticeably lovesick pair go—losing them in the crowd of drunk dancers—I realized it made perfect sense that true mates would be able to ride their dragons unsinged. It wasn't just *me*. I wasn't *special*, even if I was a hybrid. Somehow this information must have gotten buried over the years. The news needed to be shared across the dragon shifter and supernatural communities, as I couldn't imagine all the supernatural beings out there afraid to touch their shifted dragon significant others, worried that they might burn them. And Hogar's saddles and protective gear wouldn't be needed for mates to ride their dragons. That gear would only be needed for combat purposes, never for true mates.

A gentle tap on my shoulder had me turning around. I dropped my gaze to the sweetly smiling face of *Marie*, of all people. She had a bouquet of wild flowers in hand, and appeared to be in perfect health. My smile brightened. "Marie!"

In all honesty, I hadn't expected to see Aden again, but there he was, standing at a safe distance with a proud papa djinn smile on his face as his daughter gave me the bouquet. Unfortunately, the alpha hall was the *last* place a child should be right now, given the level of debauched celebrating in effect, so I took her hand and asked if she could escort me outside. The little hybrid nodded, and I met Aden's dark eyes as we walked by. The djinn fell in line behind me, and within seconds we were outside. I inhaled deeply, savoring the scent of fresh, clean air—the inside of Darius's alpha hall smelled like a club on a Saturday night.

"These are so *beautiful*," I gushed when we finally found a spot away from the inebriated victory-partiers. I took a seat on a boulder near Darius's bedroom hall, admiring each flower individually as Marie stood by, grinning and blushing. "Can you tell me the names?"

Much to my surprise, the girl named every flower in the batch, offering up their scientific classification too—as if she wasn't impressive enough. While I detected the djinn within her, whatever she was crossed with, whatever her mother had been, was a little less clear.

"Marie wanted to thank you for everything you did for us," Aden said after a long, contemplative pause had passed. I looked up, clutching the flowers tightly, and noted the strain on his features—as though holding back a tidal wave of emotion. "*I* wanted to thank you. You saved my daughter's life."

"I just did what anyone would have done—"

"I won't forget it," he assured me, moving closer and setting a hand on Marie's shoulder. His fingertips shimmered blue, and she quickly became distracted with them, laughing softly as her father conjured stars inside the mist. It was like looking at the night's sky, but in the palm of Aden's hand. When I met the djinn's eye again, I offered a small nod of understanding.

"You saved my mate," I told him, "and that's something I won't forget either."

"I'd say we were even, but that might sever our salacious bond," Aden mused, his eyes sparkling with mischief. "Let's just agree to part today as friends. Anytime you need me, you can summon me with a thought. I'll keep you on my radar."

"Maybe..." I swallowed hard, my smile softening as I studied Marie for a moment. "Maybe you could tell me a little more about hybrid lore. You seem to be an expert on it."

"I have a pretty hefty stake in the community, I suppose," he murmured as he leaned down and pressed a kiss to Marie's temple. She squirmed out of the way, her face pinched in a *yuck, Dad!* sort of way. "What would you like to know?"

I shrugged. "Is everything too much?"

The djinn chuckled, twirling a bit of Marie's dark hair around his fingers. "No, I suppose not. It's my understanding that there are, in fact, some hybrid communities in hiding today." He raised an eyebrow, as though *feeling* my excitement. "It's only a rumor, of course, but perhaps one worth exploring. After all, the artifacts were only rumors..."

"Yes, *please*." The thought of finding more hybrids like myself, of learning my actual *culture* rather than just guessing at it, was incredibly appealing. "When can we start?"

"How about tomorrow?" Darius interjected, and I stood, my cheeks reddening as he strolled toward us. I'd been so wrapped up in the idea of hybrids that I hadn't even noticed him approaching, but my inner dragon—because that's what she was, no longer just a voice—made little growl-like whimpering noises in my head, like the ones dogs made when their humans came home, at the sight of him. I shared her sentiment. Even though we'd been working together for hours at this point, I felt as though I'd hardly seen him.

Aden and Darius exchanged a few words, all pleasant, before my dragon grabbed my hand and excused us. I waved goodbye to both Aden and Marie, and although I was desperate for more intel about hybrids, I had no qualms turning my back on the festivities and following Darius into the mountains.

We walked in a companionable silence, the kind steeped with an unspoken desire for closeness, for what felt like hour. To the end of the range. To the end of the earth, it seemed. Darius and I, together at last with no one to interrupt or threaten or dampen our spirits. I held Marie's gift loosely in one hand, but clung tightly to him with my other. When we finally did stop, we stood with our toes at the edge of a steep cliff, a valley of late summer green flourishing before us. On the other side of the range, we would've seen blood, mud, and charred earth. The natural world would recover from yesterday's battle, but I knew there were supernaturals and shifters alike who might not ever.

I inhaled deeply, breathing in the cool gust of wind barreling over us, deciding right then and there to put all that out of my mind. Darius and I had earned a few hours to ourselves, unfettered by all the problems and stress waiting back at the village.

"You know, Aden said there are rumors of hybrid clans out

there," I admitted, my gaze on the horizon. Darius gave my hand a little squeeze, and I smiled. "I'd like to see if that's true."

"Whenever you're ready to go, just tell me," he said. "I'll be right by your side."

I closed my eyes for a moment, letting the weight of his words wash over me, exhaling all the negativity and darkness that had clung to me for so long.

"Thank you."

"Of course. Together, or—"

"Not at all," I finished for him, and we smiled at one another. Our gazes locked, and my breath quickened, heart fluttered, at the dark longing in his stormy grays. Slowly, carefully, Darius freed the bouquet from my grasp and set it aside somewhere safe where the wind couldn't take it. He then stood before me, towering over me as he always did, and cocked his head to the side.

"Now, Kaye my fae," he started, his voice gravelly and lips twitching into a sinful smirk that sent tingles straight to my core, "I am so proud of you for shifting, but I can't believe I missed your first time."

"Yeah, you were off in the lap of luxury getting healed," I teased. My hand found its way to the center of his chest, pushing slightly against the muscular surface as I searched for his heartbeat. Steady. Ever-constant and firm. It might just be the only thing that would help me fall asleep tonight.

His lips parted, as though about to say something, and I tensed, waiting. However, rather than saying a word, Darius swooped down and kissed me instead. My eyes fluttered closed as his lips claimed mine, a rush of white hot excitement shooting down from where we joined to the crux of my thighs.

All I wanted was him—more of him, more of what we had the night of that huge summer storm. As our lips parted, he slipped his tongue into my mouth, coaxing mine, teasing me into a little game of cat and mouse as my hands wandered his body's hardness. I giggled, the sound trapped between us, when he nipped at my lower lip, then darted back, forcing me to pursue. My hands fisted in the warm fabric of his gray T-shirt, and before I realized what I was doing, I had dragged it up and over his head. Our mouths hovered near one another, a breath away from contact, the heat of his bare torso radiating toward me. Slowly, I let my fingers wander the expansive plains of his sculpted chest, grinning at the way he twitched when I skimmed over a ticklish spot.

"I want to see you, *now*," he growled, stealing himself away when I tried to stand up on my tip-toes, throw my arms around his neck, and kiss him well into the next century. I bit my lower lip, my body humming with desire, and shook my head.

"Get back here, you."

"It's the perfect day for flying," he reasoned, and when I lunged forward, Darius caught me around the waist, hoisted me up, and pressed me back against a nearby rock. I arched against him, pleased with the change of positions, but rather than meet me halfway, my lips aching for the dangerous caress of his, my dragon snagged my shirt and yanked it off too. I steadied myself, allowing him to undress me, and watched as he took his time. There were no torn panties, no ripped jeans. He handled each item of clothing with care—that is, until it came to his own.

As I stood there, totally naked, the wind whispering over my exposed skin, Darius took a few steps back and all but shredded the rest of his clothes in an effort to get them off. They landed next to mine in a disorganized pile, and I bit my cheeks to keep from blushing at the sight of his very prominent... *interest* in our activities. He held out his hand, inching toward the edge of the cliff with a smile. "Come on, sweetheart. Show me your wings."

I swallowed hard, knowing he understood the impact of me finally having my own wings. I'd always wanted to be able to fly, but only a few faes were blessed with the ability. Now, in theory, I could fly anywhere I wanted.

So why did the idea make my stomach flip-flop and my palms sweat?

"I... I don't know if I *can* fly," I told him shyly. "I mean, I sort of just chased Jasmine around. I know they work, I just don't know if I can... do it."

How depressing would *that* be? I'd waited all this time, and then my wings don't work? Or I just couldn't figure out how to manage them?

"Put some faith in yourself, Kaye," Darius insisted, and I suddenly noticed he was all but hanging off the edge of the cliff, his heels creeping over the side. "She won't let you fall..."

"She?"

"You know who I'm talking about." And then, grinning like a fool, he held his arms out and fell backward over the edge. My first instinct was to panic; shrieking, I screamed his name and raced to the edge—only to stumble backward as Darius's dragon form raced by me. I laughed, a blend of relief and anger rushing through my system, as I watched him soar above, his sunset red and orange scales exquisite against the baby blue backdrop. He issued a low, long roar, as though beckoning me to join him. That feeling returned, the sensation of my insides fluttering about, shifting beneath my skin. Although I couldn't hear her, I knew my inner dragon was still there, waiting in the magical recesses of my body—eager to stretch her wings.

Swallowing hard, I sidled over to the edge and peered down. It was a long, steep drop, with nothing but boulders and jagged rocks at the bottom.

"Don't let me splat, okay?" My voice shook as I turned and mirrored Darius's stance, my heels creeping over the edge. Adrenaline pounded through me, spiking hard as I closed my eyes, held out my arms, and threw caution to the wind.

I let myself fall.

For a moment, the freefall forced my heart into my throat, and the scream that slipped free did so of its own accord. It felt like hours of falling, but it couldn't have been more than a few seconds before my human-esque features started to elongate, my skin turning coarse and green. This time, there was no popping of joints and cracking of bones. In a blink, my vision went from ordinary to extraordinary, the sharpness of my dragon's view coming into swift focus.

And I didn't have to think. I reacted to the moment, rolling my unfamiliar—yet distinctly comfortable—dragon's body over in midair. My wings snapped into motion, stretching out and instantly slowing my descent. I sailed through the air, far above the ground, and with a slight roll of my shoulders, my wings flapped.

My excited cry echoed across the valley, and I looked up as a shadow passed overhead. Darius. Seeing him in my dragon form, the bond between us was glaringly obvious. I'd never felt more comfortable, more familiar, and more at home with anyone, in any form, in all my life. Somehow, it was like I knew him *more* in this form, like we had been mates a thousand times over, in a thousand different lives. Nostalgia bubbled through me—nostalgia and love, as though seeing him now was like happening upon a long-lost lover who I'd been searching for across time.

He soared above me, then cut down sharply and looped around me. I hazarded a dive myself, closing my eyes for a moment when my wings snapped out and sent me arcing upward again.

We carried on like that for some time, exploring one another as best we could in the air. Chasing each other. Soaring over the mountain range. Looping around one another, snapping at tails as they passed, our roars a single song carrying over the landscape. Finally, we turned outward, away from the village and its mountain home. Side by side, we climbed higher and higher, dipping in and out of clouds, and flew with no purpose, no real destination in mind. We sought out the infinite horizon, with its endless possibilities and its hope for a better, brighter tomorrow.

One that we would seek out together...

Or not at all.

～

Thank you for reading **MAGIC BLAZE!**

Want more Shifter Romance? Check out my **Shifter Alphas Furever Series**:

Claimed by Her Two Alphas
Claimed by Her Wolf
Claimed by Her Bear
Claimed by Her Dragon

GET A FREE SEDONA VENEZ BOOK!

https://sedonavenez.com/free-book

WANT FREE SEDONA VENEZ BOOKS?

Sign up for Sedona Venez's Newsletter and receive FREE BOOKS. In addition to the free stories, you will also get special pricing, exclusive previews and news of new releases.

GET A FREE SEDONA VENEZ BOOK!

Join Sedona's mailing list to be the first to know of new releases, free books, special prices and other author giveaways.

https://sedonavenez.com/free-book

ABOUT THE AUTHOR

USA TODAY BESTSELLING AUTHOR SEDONA VENEZ lives in New York City with her hot ex-military hubby—hooah—and their fur babies. She loves writing sizzling, sexy intricate stories about strong but broken characters who push limits, overcome their fears and risk it all for love.

Sedona loves to connect with readers!
www.sedonavenez.com